*The Abyssinian Mountain Lion & other stories*

To Kristan + Rob
with my love +
Best wishes to
You future back
in: Canada.

# The Abyssinian
# Mountain Lion
# & other stories

DAVID MCDOUGALL

will miss you
David.!

submarine

First published in 2015

Typeset by Paul Stewart
Edited by Mary McCallum
Design by Mākaro Press

Cover image: John McDougall
Author photo: Simon Hoyle, Southlight

ISBN 978-0-9941069-9-5

A catalogue record for this book is available from the
National Library of New Zealand

Printed by Printstop,
Wellington, New Zealand

Submarine
an imprint of Mākaro Press
PO Box 41-032 Eastbourne 5047
makaropress.co.nz

*For my dearest Jude,*
*and all our lovely family.*

# The Abyssinian Mountain Lion

We'd spent a long, interesting, exhausting day, changing trains three times from Barcelona to Florence. Tiredness encouraged us to book a pension at an information kiosk in the railway station concourse. We chose the easy option which was within walking distance, but it was a mistake. Our room on the first floor faced a main road. The noise of motorcycles, cars, trucks and buses made sleeping difficult, and vehicle fumes wafted through badly fitting window frames causing headaches and vague feelings of nausea. But in another way our accommodation was fortuitous – it led us to again choose the easiest option, a small cheap restaurant on the ground floor of the same building. We were hungry as well as tired, so we looked no further than this modest establishment frequented by working-class locals.

We were seated at a table facing the door, having

just ordered a meal, when I looked up from examining the cleanliness of my cutlery to see an old man walk in through the door. He had a compact, slightly rotund body, and a long face with muscular cheeks and a tight little mouth.

'Look, Rosemary,' I said. 'It's Robert Muldoon's cousin.' Rosemary, who was giving the wine list her expert attention, agreed the likeness to our past prime minister was unmistakeable. Here was a smaller, slightly fairer, and, judging by his expression, sadder edition of Muldoon.

My gaze switched to the waiter. He was tall and somewhat arrogant, but professional in the way he had taken our order without needing to write it down, memorising every detail. I watched as he acknowledged what appeared to be a regular patron, nodding to 'Muldoon' who returned the gesture. The waiter then began moving a small table alongside ours. The old man stood staring at the ceiling while this was going on.

Muldoon seated himself and the waiter took his order. I guessed he said in Italian something like, 'The usual?' The waiter retreated and within minutes returned with bread and a bowl of minestrone, which he placed with considerable care in front of Muldoon. Almost immediately the man turned to speak to us: 'Excuse me, I notice you are speaking Eng-lish. Where are you from, if you please?' He presented himself as polite and smiling – slightly timorous.

'We're from New Zealand,' said Rosemary tapping

the New Zealand flag button she wore on her lapel.

'Ahh, that is good, and what part of New Zea-land may I enquire?'

'From Wellington.'

It was now clear to me what the furniture moving was about. The waiter was accustomed to accommodating the patron's wish to practice his English.

'Ah, from Well-ing-ton.' He had a tendency to stretch certain words, otherwise his English was perfect. 'That is very inter-resting, from Well-ing-ton. I lived in Well-ing-ton for a year, a long time ago, in 1955. I held a temporary lectureship in the Italian depart-ament at Victoria University. Do you know Victoria University?'

'Yes, yes, of course. We are both familiar with the university,' I said.

Rosemary spoke up, 'Actually, I taught at Victoria for ten years, in the geography department.'

But Muldoon, who was crumbling his bread and had just taken a sip of the minestrone, was more inter-ested in his own story. 'I lived in a small apar-tment in Newtown, Mansfield Street, near the zoo. I would catch a tramcar into the city, and then the cable car to the University. Does the cable car still run?'

'It was replaced several years ago with a modern one, but yes it's still operating,' I said.

'I was very unhappy in Well-ing-ton, nobody be-friended me. I was left to my own devices, as you say. Even the people in the depart-ament preferred to ignore me, the others were all Italian-speaking Kiwis.'

As he spoke he used the back of his hand to wipe away the tears that had run down his muscular cheeks.

I was thinking back to Wellington in the mid-fifties, especially the attitudes toward foreigners at that time. The old man was of a very serious disposition and not at all like the ebullient Italian stereotype. Back then he would have been labelled a 'sober-sides', and possibly a depressive, as indeed he appeared to be now. I remembered well the anti-foreigner attitudes and the casual racial slurs. Any Italian would have been referred to as a 'Wop', 'Dago' or the somewhat milder term, 'Itie'.

He went on to ask why we had come to Firenze.

'We'll be revisiting some of the popular classical sites,' said Rosemary, speaking in a gentle voice. 'We've been here several times over the years. First we would like to spend a day at the Uffizi Gallery, though. In particular we would like to reacquaint ourselves with the Vermeers we have so admired previously.'

'Ah, that will not be possible, I am afraid. That section of the Gallery is closed. I understand it is for political purposes. The Directors, it is rumoured, want more government funding for the entire Gallery. They believe that by closing that part of the Uffizi, claiming they have insufficient resources to keep this most popular section open, the art-loving population of our country will put pressure on the government. Do you understand what I am saying?'

'Yes, to be sure.' Our primary reason for coming all this way had been stymied. I felt annoyed and somewhat saddened. I believe my mood was influenced by the old man's demeanour.

'You were not happy with the way you were treated in Wellington all those years ago. Did you not make any friends at all?' asked Rosemary.

'Not really. I am not an outgoing person, which would not have helped. I did make what I like to think of as a friend, though. The zoo was near where I lived and I spent quite a lot of my time there talking to the ani-mals.'

I was tempted to ask whether he spoke to the animals in Italian or English.

'I made a very special friend of one particular ani-mal. The lions' cages were close to the entrance, and on my first visit I found one cage which housed a solitary female lion that was quite a lot smaller than the other lions. There was a sign on her cage which said "Abyssinian Mountain Lion". She was such a beautiful creature, as are all lions, but this one looked so sad. I thought to myself, how wrong for her to be so far from her home in Abyssinia, which as you will know is now called Ethiopia. But there was something else which drew me to "Mistress", which was my name for her.'

Rosemary edged her chair closer to the old gentleman. I could see she was as intrigued as I was. We seemed to have temporarily forgotten our tiredness.

He continued. 'You may remember the fascist dictator Mussolini who caused the Italian people so much trouble and heartache. *Il Duce* had ambitions, and part of that was to have a colonial empire. He invaded

Abyssinia in 1935 with his army of largely conscripted soldiers. The Italian people had little stomach for war. My father was one of those conscripted soldiers. I was a very small boy and my memories of him are vague. But I know I loved my father very much, and I have always thought of him and imagined that he loved me as well. He died of a tropical disease, and his remains are buried somewhere out in North East Africa. I have tried to find his grave, but without success.

'And so I imagined I had a connection to my lost father through this poor, sad, beautiful Abyssinian mountain lion, Mistress. I went so often to visit my lion that I believed she recognised me as a friend. When she saw me approach her cage she would walk toward me, and stand close to the bars of her prison. I used to talk to her about my sadness and loneliness and she seemed to understand. I think it helped me – talking to her like that. When I left New Zealand after only one year, I felt very guilty about abandoning my friend.'

The poor man was so utterly involved in telling this story he had completely forgotten about his minestrone.

'That is indeed a sad story,' I said. 'If you were to visit New Zealand now, I'm sure you would be treated very differently. There are many Italian people living in Wellington, valued members of our community, lots of them successful business people, in the fisheries and restaurant industries in particular. A great number of Kiwis visit Italy now, many of them trying to learn a smattering of your language.'

'I know,' he said, 'I have met a few here in this restaurant, quite often young people who want to practice their language skills on me, while I am wanting to talk to them in En-glish.'

I had been feeling just a little responsible for my countrymen's attitudes toward him all those years ago. 'If you ever consider coming to New Zealand for a holiday you would find it quite different – our attitude to foreigners, I mean. We are rapidly becoming a multi-cultural society. If you like I'll give you our address – we have a spare bed, if you do ever come.'

'That is very generous of you, but no I couldn't leave my cat. I don't trust anybody else to feed her. And of course Mistress, my beautiful mountain lion, she would have died many, many years ago – quite probably from a broken heart.'

With that, he withdrew an ancient pocket watch and placed it on the table, bending his large oval head over it, peering short-sightedly at the time. I guessed the watch might have belonged to his father. He snapped it shut and stood up, having eaten very little of his bread and soup.

'Thank you for listening to me, I like to practise my En-glish. But now I must go, Mistress will be waiting for her dinner.' And he scuttled toward the door. Other than the physical appearance, there was none of the Muldoon confidence and swagger about the old chap.

We had hardly noticed the taste or quality of the food we'd been eating. Muldoon's mood, his story, and the news about the Uffizi left us feeling deflated.

'Let's find a bar,' said Rosemary. 'All that feline anthropomorphism is fine, but I need a drink. After all, this is a holiday is it not?'

# You Ironed my Shorts
## for Saint Valentine

I'm sitting on the edge of the bed inspecting my socks, when she calls from the kitchen: 'I've ironed your shorts!'

'What's that?' I say. 'You shouldn't have worried. Thanks anyway.' I don't mind them not ironed. What I really mean is, if I'd had to iron them myself, I wouldn't have bothered.

'Pooh!' I've passed the socks under my nose, while listening carefully to make sure she's not about to enter the room. I'd be in trouble if she caught me. I pull them on.

'It's your St Valentine's Day present,' She's got a low-register voice, so she bellows. She says she has to because I'm deaf. She's the deaf one, I reckon.

'Is it? I mean is it St Valentine's Day? That's very nice of you, with all you've got on, ironing my shorts and

I haven't got you a thing.' My conscience pricks – she loves flowers, but I block out that idea.

Years ago there was a brief affair, one of the girls at the office, actually it was *her* office, come to think of it. It only happened once, I swear. But the light of my life found out *after* I brought home the flowers. Next time I got her some, she suspected I'd been up to a bit of mischief again. Accusations led to one helluva row. So that was the last time. Now she keeps telling friends I never buy her flowers, which puts me in a complete double bind.

'I can't win,' I blurt out.

'What's that?' She calls out.

'Nothing. Got a busy day?' I already know the answer – all her days are busy. I can hear her moving round the kitchen putting things away.

'Busy all right. I'm leading a three-hour seminar, then a meeting with the board, and a report to finish, and I think I might have a flaming migraine coming on.'

'Why on earth don't you take a sickie for once?'

She doesn't reply. I can't remember when she last had a day off.

'Wow!' I say. 'You're looking sexy.'

She's come into the room, collecting her bag and keys. 'Look, I must be off, my love … what are you doing today?'

'Nothing planned – may go for a swim later. Looks like a nice day.'

Here she is, working her guts out and I'm talking about going to the pool. All that activity, and absolutely no sympathy for the delicate state of my conscience.

'Must fly – see you later.' She rushes toward the door, pausing to proffer a cheek instead of the customary lips. 'Have you changed your socks lately?' It's the last thing I hear as she exits.

Phew! She's gone. I do worry about her, though. How long can she keep that pace up? St Valentines, St Valentines. I'll surprise her tonight. Obviously flowers are out.

'A poem perhaps? What'd you think, Bozo?' I'm talking to the dog again. Is that better than talking to yourself? Come to think of it, I do quite a lot of that as well. 'Here it is:

'You ironed my shorts for Saint Valentine.
No mean feat considering your commitments –
giving yourself beyond the call …'

That came easily enough. It occurs to me that 'no mean feat' feels a bit close to 'smelly feet'. Another idea comes to mind. A cake might do the trick, a banana cake. I heard her saying recently about banana being her favourite. Meanwhile I have another go at the poem (out loud):

'You ironed my shorts for Saint Valentine.
No mean feat considering your commitments –
giving yourself beyond the call.
I gave you nothing, but resolved
to clean the house come Friday.'

Why did I drop that line in about house cleaning? Sooner rather than later she'll be looking around and commenting on the state of the house. But if I put it in, I'm committed. I loathe doing housework.

I find a recipe for banana cake, several in fact, decide on the one that looks the simplest. I'm checking to see whether we've got all the ingredients: bananas, eggs, butter, flour, vanilla. Yes, got all that.

'For God's sake, dog, get out of the kitchen!' I'll have to stop feeding that mutt. Every time I go into the kitchen, he's there watching me, all swoony-eyed. 'Here, have a biscuit and take it outside. Outside! *Outside!* God, you're hopeless.'

I cobble the ingredients together, taking great care to measure everything *exactly*. This sort of enterprise always takes far longer than I anticipate. I shove it into the oven setting the timer at fifty minutes. 'Damn!' I've forgotten to switch the oven on. At this rate, I'll miss the 11.30 bus. She wouldn't have a clue how busy I am some days. While the cake is baking, I change into my shorts, admiring the creases, a clean shirt and my running shoes – could be I'll need those to sprint for the bus. Just a little time to spend on the poem. I could substitute the banana cake for the housework.

'… I gave you nothing, but made
a banana cake – your favourite.'

No, think I'll stick with 'cleaning the house come Friday'. I'll get around to it sooner or later – have to –

but *Friday?* Early retirement wasn't such a good idea.

'Expressions of devotion …'

Yeah, that's it:

> '… and a trillion other small gifts since our vows,
> measured against which we haven't done badly
> these thirty-eight years – speaking for myself.'

There's a ring of sincerity about it, I'll leave it at that.

*Ding, ding, ding, ding, ding, ding!*

Oven. I'm getting the cake out when I catch something on the news. The deputy leader, my erstwhile hero, now but a fallen idol openly challenging the PM in parliament. This coalition is doomed. Jesus! If I stop to listen, I really will miss the bus.

I fling myself out the back door. The wind has swung my togs against the fence, and they're hooked on a nail. 'Come here!' I reach up and yank them free. 'Gotcha.'

Back in the kitchen, I catch the dog with his paws up on the bench. He's sniffing the cake and salivating like crazy. He'll be up there eating it soon as my back's turned. I slam it into the pantry. 'Here, have a biscuit. Yes, I'll take you walkies later. You're in charge, Bozo. See yah!' I catapult out the door.

I'm running for the bus, hailing the driver who pulls up fifty metres past the stop.

'Good on yer, mate! I didn't fancy waiting an hour for the next one. Wai-iti Crescent please!'

Standing on the diving board, I admit I've been showing off a bit. I used to be good at this but let's face it, my technique's not up to much these days. But that woman in the red bathing suit with the great boobs, breaststroking up and down the lanes, she's been smiling at me, egging me on, I reckon.

Haven't done a tuck one-and-a-half back 'somie', for quite some time. I swivel around on the balls of my feet, arms out in front, elbows braced. I'm about to spring into action when I spot the young blonde pool attendant – she's a looker too. She's standing just back from the other end of the board, holding out a towel and beckoning me.

'Excuse me, sir.' Perhaps she thinks I'm in some sort of danger, diving at my age. 'Sir, there's been a complaint – well not really a complaint – that ah, your ah, privates are clearly visible when you're standing on the end of the board.'

'Shit!' My hand shoots down. I must have ripped the togs when I dragged them off the fence. That's the problem with having poetry and banana cakes and that bloody dog on my brain all at once – too much to cope with.

I shuffle off the board, and she hands me the towel to wrap around myself. By this time, the woman in the red bathing suit is out of the water and she's standing alongside us as well. This obviously calls for an apology.

'I'm terribly sorry for that er … display. I assure you, I'm not into exposing myself. I mean, I'm not like those dirty old men who leap out of the bushes.'

I go on with a full explanation of how I was in danger of missing the bus, how I'd found my togs hooked on the neighbour's fence and ripped them off the nail in my rush. The pool attendant is standing there politely, looking ever so demure, while 'red bathing suit' has a broad grin on her face, and is obviously suppressing a giggle.

I turn to her. 'Did you tip this young lady off about … you know …'

'Oh, good heavens, no. I would be the last person to spoil the show for all the other women in the pool.'

'Well,' I say good-naturedly, 'You're a saucy so-and-so.'

I get changed, and emerge fully dressed. She's there, standing by the entrance, also fully dressed. She looks even better than she did in the bathing suit.

'I wonder if you'd like a coffee after all that excite-ment. I know a nice little place not far from here,' she says. 'My car's right there in the carpark. I could run you to your bus stop after we've had a cuppa and a little chat.'

Of course, being a true gentleman, I agree, on con-dition I pay for her coffee. Five minutes later we're seated at a cosy little place. Jill, that's her name, asks me about the diving caper, and how often I go to the pool. Turns out she's pretty much a regular – swims laps to keep fit.

'I don't think you were as embarrassed as you should have been in the circumstances,' she said. 'I caught an element of pride in the old, you know, "wedding tackle". I assume you *are* married, as am I.'

We have a friendly chat, with Jill still laughing at my predicament. She's going to dine out on that little number for quite a while, I suspect. She kindly gets me to the bus stop with a couple of minutes to spare.

'See you at the pool,' she says.

I get home and start in on the housework. If I get at least some of it done, I can reward myself walking Bozo.

# Lillian

Lillian's thinking of getting her hair cut, one of those modern shorter styles, what a relief that would be. But perhaps not – such a drastic step. Stanley would never approve. She catches her reflection in the bus window. Her hair is thinner now, but remarkably still retains much of its golden colour. She wears it in a roll framing her face, tucked under a folded silk scarf knotted at the neck, much as she wore it during the war. Heavens, she thinks, that would be all of thirty years ago. Lillian was once secretly proud of her hair, and her blue eyes, lively eyes, set in a face admired for its bone structure, but now rather plump. It no longer matters.

She's sitting on the bus wondering how the film ended. Missing the ending is a regular occurrence these days. There was a time when Lillian would go to the matinees several times a week, but now it was once only. There's a new interest in her life.

At Courtenay Place the young couple is waiting to board. They've been on her mind since they sat in front of her last week. There's something comfortably familiar, and attractive about this couple, but she can't quite put her finger on what it is. Could it be the shy interest they take in each other? It's setting her thinking about herself and Stanley in their youth, in those months they'd shared when their love for each other was new, exciting, romantic. He was full of confidence then.

She smiles as she remembers his wry sense of humour, and the little practical jokes they played on each other. Like the time he gave her a pair of nylon stockings which he said he'd secured from an American serviceman 'with connections'. When she unwrapped the little parcel she found they were laddered and full of holes. Her mouth opened in disbelief as she fought to hold back tears. After comforting her he'd then produced another packet with the real thing – *two* pairs of nylons! She'd burst out crying and laughing at the same time. So often they laughed together.

Lillian asks herself for the umpteenth time whether she still loves him, what sort of marriage it has been, what kept them together all these years. Things are quite different now. They were carefree then despite being on the brink of that great abyss. What they have now is certainly nothing like the couple on the bus. She studies them as they stand beside the driver, the young man is paying both their fares.

They are both slim and dark, and he is a head taller, which means she has to look up at him. Peter, the name Lillian's given him. He looks down in an adoring protective way at Chloe. Yes, that name fits her well. Peter looks sensitive, but when he smiles his face lights up. It's the way he smiles, she now realises, that reminds her of Stanley. The way Stanley was. She'll describe Peter's smile in the story she's going to write about them. Lillian wants to become a writer, has already started in fact. This is her secret. No one, not even Stanley or the children, or any of her friends, knows about this new interest in her life.

Lillian's writing began when they changed the time-table, discontinued the 3.45. That was the one which got her home in time to get Stanley's dinner on the table sharp at 5.30, ten minutes after arriving from his own bus. Strict adherence to meal times is the thing she loathes most about their unvarying routine.

Lillian has a love affair with the movies. Three, sometimes four afternoons a week since the children left home, she's indulged her passion. Both her favourite cinemas start their afternoon programmes at two. She sits in that darkened, familiar, flickering fantasy world, living the lives of the movie people. She'll watch anything, but prefers the romantic ones, re-runs of old films – Bogart and Bacall, Catherine Hepburn, Joseph Cotton, Ingrid Bergman, Spencer Tracy, Joan Crawford, and the elegant, wonderfully romantic dancing of Astaire and Rodgers. The burden of the constant attention to Stanley's needs lifts by the time she emerges into the sunlight, heading for her bus.

Stanley has no idea how important these matinees are, or how often she goes. There was a time when, over the dinner table, she'd sometimes tell him about a film she'd seen. He made the right noises, pretending to listen, but his eyes would glaze over, or he'd get up and turn on the TV, or unthinkingly interrupt her story in some other way.

At the cinema, Lillian always chooses the seat nearest the exit so she can slip out without causing a disturbance. It came to her once that the usher may have wondered whether she was claustrophobic. Nowadays she has to catch the 3.15 – the 4.15 would be too late to have Stanley's dinner on the table when he walks in.

Lillian could have asked if Stanley minded having his meal half an hour later, and he might have agreed, but she'd have seen again the haunted look, his fear of the shattering nightmares returning. The whole of his life has to be meticulously ordered. There are the obsessions she must indulge, too, like the statistics he keeps and continually fiddles with: all the major cricket and rugby games going right back to the year dot. Always collecting and ordering those dates, scores and averages, which he wears like chain mail. They both know, but never openly acknowledge, that this is a necessary way to ward off the fear of the memories, and those terrible, terrible nightmares where he wakes screaming and sweating, quite disoriented. Any amount of routine is better than the threat his life would fly apart.

Stanley is unaware that for the past twelve months Lillian has not seen the end of even one of her beloved movies. Sitting on the 3.15, twenty minutes before the film she's watched is due to finish, she has begun composing her own endings. Then she's started writing them down the following day; and now she's beginning to write complete stories, like the one she plans to write about the young couple sitting directly behind her. Lillian is intrigued by snippets of their conversation. It seems Chloe is a student of music, while Peter does something at the hospital, his current shift starting at 6.30am.

*It's the First World War in a field hospital close to the front-line. Peter is the unflappable surgeon operating under extreme conditions, assisted by Chloe a nurse recently posted to the unit. He makes jokes to relieve the tension while they work, and often whistles snatches of classical music. That's what brings them together. Chloe has her violin with her and she plays for him some evenings. They have already fallen in love when a bursting mortar shell wounds Peter. Chloe patches him up so he can finish the operation he's performing. After that he collapses, and she nurses him back to health.*

Lillian plans to expand this theme. What particularly excites her is the way the young couple talk, the warmth with which they address each other, the gentleness in their voices. She's quite sure they're in love, it's obvious, and she can't help wondering whether they share the same bed. They probably do, she decides. Don't all young couples these days? Lillian smiles as she recalls how long ago, after Stanley enlisted, and during their short engagement, they made love frequently. There was an urgency about it, so little time to enjoy each other.

They spent magical afternoons in a flat belonging to a friend of Stanley's. He'd kindly lent them a key and said they could use the place whenever he was away. They would lower the blinds, dance to romantic music on the gramophone, then, very slowly, undress each other. Some afternoons they'd be tearing each other's clothes off before they were properly inside the door.

Lillian wonders whether Stanley ever thinks about that pretty little flat, and the way the afternoon sun filtered through the wooden slats. She'd thought of asking but decided against it, there is a possibility he may not remember. Lillian stifles the idea.

How would she write a love scene about these young people? How explicit should it be, or should she merely hint at their lovemaking? She didn't favour a metaphorical approach. No, it would be delicately done, and much, much more erotic than those steamy encounters in the popular literature.

Lillian hasn't told a soul, particularly Stanley, about never seeing the end of a film these days. Certainly not the children, they are always so intolerant of his funny little ways, of his need for constant routine in his life. They would criticise, and say he was a tyrant or some such thing, and she can't bear that. He isn't a tyrant, she thinks. But she's been questioning herself about a lot of things lately. No, Stanley isn't like that at all, always so appreciative of anything she does for him. It isn't Stanley who's made her life so frustrating, so circumscribed. She mustn't blame him. It was the war, the war changed everything – she must hold on to that. *She must.*

Sitting on the bus, nearing her stop she's thinking about the exercise books hidden behind a stack of towels in the linen cupboard. Tomorrow morning she'll start a story about a young couple during the First World War. She can hardly wait to begin.

But how to end? That will have to wait, she can't yet decide.

# The Reefer Jacket

On the evening of the party Doug messed around, making sure they'd arrive late. He'd been racking his brains for days trying to find an excuse for not going at all. He hadn't told Rachael about his suspicions, the sniggers and sly looks that passed around the lunch room whenever Charles's private life was mentioned. He had this half-formed belief that if he talked about something like *that*, it would somehow cause it to happen.

Doug had very mixed feelings when he saw Rachael done up for the party; excitement and dread dwelt in the pit of his stomach. She looked lovely in the little black dress. Rachael had the sexiest legs and those turquoise stockings with the spangles showed them off a treat. He managed to restrain himself from commenting on the shortness of her dress, and the rather revealing neckline. He knew from experience it wouldn't be worth upsetting her. At the very last moment it occurred to him to suggest they forget the party altogether. They could light the fire and settle down for the evening, just the two of them. But then Rachael loved parties, and she was right, he couldn't afford to snub the boss.

Charles and Maggie were welcoming, and seemed genuinely pleased to see Doug and Rachael.

'Nice bit of cloth, Dougie,' said Charles fingering the lapel of Doug's brand new reefer jacket.

'Yeah, it cost a bomb,' said Doug.

Rachael spoke up. 'I said to Doug, it's an investment, a jacket like that. The man in the shop said jackets like that never go out of fashion. Don't you agree, Charles?'

'I'm sure you're right, Ruth.'

'Rachael's the name,' said Doug noticing Charles focusing on his wife's turquoise legs, in fact appraising her from head to toe. Doug loved Rachael's warm, friendly nature, but it sometimes created problems when she acted without thinking. He'd been worrying about that since the invitation. Something could go awry in a situation like this. He had a cautious nature – was always taking his time to make decisions, and referred to in the family as 'careful old Doug'.

Maggie whisked Rachael away, the two of them chattering like old friends, and Charles introduced Doug to some of his friends, none of whom he'd met previously. He was surprised none of the work crowd was there. He knew he was a little slow on the uptake, he'd often been teased about that, but it didn't take him long to suss out what was going on. As warehouse manager he liked things to be orderly, to be in their proper places, but this was hardly the case here. Two of the women were sitting on the laps of guys whose surnames didn't tally with their own. Alison Bruce was sitting on Geoff Stevenson's knee, Barbara Stevenson was on Frank McCartney's lap, while Sonia McCartney was cuddling on the couch with Dave Bruce. Doug arranged his face into a fixed smile.

Other couples were dancing to the slow, sexy music; in fact, they were really just swaying, hardly moving at all. The lights were dimmed right down. Standing on the sideline Doug caught a whiff of sweat mingled with the women's perfume. He gripped the handle of the beer mug the boss had armed him with, and thrust his other hand into the pocket of the reefer jacket, exactly as he'd seen Prince Charles do on television. He was sure his tie was right for the occasion, red and blue stripes, which could be regimental. Or perhaps it looked more nautical. As he lowered his eyes to admire the splendid creases in his grey flannel trousers, he reflected on the casual dress of the other men, open-necked shirts and black skivvies, not another reefer jacket in sight.

The jacket gave him confidence, it fitted perfectly and the silky lining had a luxurious feel to it. Doug stood there gently rocking on the balls of his feet, and caught a glimpse of himself in a large mirror on the opposite wall. With his flattened nose and broad shoulders, he imagined himself as an ex-welterweight champ. Yeah, I could easily pass for a retired scrapper, he thought.

A good-looking woman was sitting by herself on the other side of the room sipping a drink. I reckon she's been eyeing me, thought Doug, every time she raises her glass to those luscious lips. To be honest, Doug had spotted her as soon as they'd arrived. How could he not have noticed those dark lustrous eyes, shoulder-length hair, the perky breasts, and trim little body. She's Asian, he thought, perhaps Filipino. Her pink dress had buttons all the way down the front, and several of the bottom ones were undone, allowing the dress to fall open right up to her smooth brown thighs. Doug could see some inner thigh and just a hint of white lace. Struth, he thought. If there's one thing turns me on!

'How's the beer?' Charles appeared at his side. 'Attractive isn't she?'

Charles doesn't miss a thing, thought Doug. But I'm not being that obvious am I? He drained the rest of his beer, and switched to searching the room for Rachael. A poncey -looking joker was leaning over her and seemed to be asking for a dance. Charles's next remark distracted Doug from something that would have usually raised his anxiety several notches.

'Attractive, all right, and unattached. Yes, Marilyn separated around the middle of last year. I reckon her husband must have been crazy going off with another woman. Probably couldn't handle Marilyn's sexual demands. She's reputed to be a man-eater, quite insatiable, I understand.'

'Is that right?' said Doug in the vaguest voice he could muster. Geez, Charles! Did he have to say that? How the hell am I to handle this situation now? His knees were trembling as blood rushed to his head and belly all at once. He hadn't felt like this in years. Charles was rabbiting on. He was such a friendly guy, not at all like some of the bosses he'd worked for. Doug was trying to concentrate enough on what Charles was saying so as to make the odd intelligent response, but he was distracted by what he was pretty sure were the smouldering looks aimed in his direction.

Charles ducked off to attend to another guest, and that's when Doug saw Rachael dancing with the poncey creep. Hey, get your mitts off my wife! The bastard had one arm round her neck playing with her hair, and the other hand was firmly stuck to her lovely bottom. Doug manoeuvred between the swaying couples and tapped the guy on his shoulder. 'Excuse me, squire.'

And so he reclaimed her.

They'd only done one turn round the floor when the same cheeky sod tapped Doug on the shoulder, edging him aside. The creep now had both arms around Rachael pulling her in, clamping her firmly amidships. That's when Doug saw red. He stepped up to the jerk, spun him round, lifted him up by the waist, upwards and backwards. *Slam!* He hit the nearest wall making the pictures rattle. It was like Doug had tossed a bale of Pink Batts from the loading bay onto the back of a truck. The guy slumped down onto a chair as a couple of women started fussing around him. It was not like he was hurt, just winded and a bit shocked.

They were all staring at Doug. Someone switched off the music. Charles suggested they turn it on again.

Doug was horrified. My God, what have I done? he thought. What did I do that for? This isn't my usual form. Nobody's coming near me, not even Rachael. She'll be so embarrassed. People don't behave like that at these sorts of parties. That's public bar stuff, not what one does at a friend's place, especially not the boss's. Shit I've blown it now. *What an idiot!* Bloody Rachael, what was she thinking of letting that bastard hold her like that?

Doug was breaking into a cold sweat.

Rachael was dancing with Charles. What was going on? Did Charles think she needed rescuing, distracting from her husband's uncouth behaviour … or perhaps he had less than honourable things on his mind. Did he think Rachael was some sort of pushover? Anyone but the boss, he thought, and I'd have her out of here in a flash.

It was clear to Doug he was being ignored. Punished for being such a dick-head. All those superior bastards treating me like I don't exist, he thought, one great big fat embarrassment. Well, fuck them! Strong language said to himself, and unusual for Doug who seldom swore.

Finding the darkest corner of the room, he sat down to try and regain his composure, and get his head around what to do next. He hadn't completely forgotten Marilyn. What on earth would *she* be thinking? He couldn't bring himself to look in her direction.

Rachael's ignoring me – still dancing with Charles, the bastard. The silly bitch, can't she see she's the cause of what's happened? If she hadn't let that creep fondle her like that … I'll go, just leave them all to root each other to death. As for Rachael, she can get herself home in a taxi.

He was almost at the front door when he felt a hand on his elbow. As Marilyn looked up at him all the unsettling feelings returned. He was about to say something when she reached up and placed her forefinger over his lips. 'Don't say anything. You follow me – I live next door.' Doug remembered later, that finger had a harshness about it, not like Rachael's.

Whoa, what was happening? His heart was pumping like mad. Thank God she's not expecting me to say anything.

Marilyn opened her front door and took his arm. He smelt an exotic perfume as her hair brushed the sleeve of his jacket. His knees were so weak he could barely manage to shuffle down her passageway. She steered him into a lounge with a large couch and a couple of easy chairs. Doug positioned himself at one end of the couch hoping Marilyn will snuggle up beside him, but when he looked around she'd vanished. He examined the room. It was almost bare except for the furniture and a standard lamp in one corner. No pictures, no books, no magazines. Easy to keep tidy; Doug liked that. Hope the anti-perspirant's still working, he thought.

Finally Marilyn put her head around the door. 'You like tea or coffee? I got some nice jasmine tea.'

I'm not being offered chilled white wine, thought Doug. 'Ah, tea please, ordinary, milk and one sugar.' Marilyn disappeared again but her perfume lingered.

She's taking an age. Perhaps she changing into a negligee or something, thought Doug. That's usually what happens in these situations. This waiting's making me feel a bit panicky, not sure I'm up to this sort of thing, especially having just made such a frigging idiot of myself next door. I'm not usually into this sort of thing at all.

Doug huffed into his hand, testing his breath, straightened his tie and unbuttoned the reefer jacket. Ah, the jacket. The thought of it comforted him enormously.

At last, Marilyn returned with the tea. She was still fully clothed … Doug was disappointed, and just a little relieved to see she'd done up all the buttons down the front of her dress. That could be signalling something. She handed Doug a cup of tea and sat down in one of the chairs.

'Charles and Maggie's parties are over the top – no? For me anyway. Not that I don't like them, and they been very good to me. I thought you were terrific the way you fix that man. What he was doing just like my husband at parties. How's the tea?'

'Just right, thanks.'

'Which bring me to why I ask you over. I don't know many men, certainly no one as tough and strong as you.'

Doug felt his chest swell.

'Back home where I come from, if my husband unfaithful I get my brothers and cousins sort him out. Do you get what I'm saying?'

'You mean you want me to go and beat the living daylights out of your husband? Whoa! Sorry, I couldn't do that. That sort of thing's illegal in this country.'

'But no one know. He never recognise you again if you wear stocking over your face. I give you one of mine.'

That part of the arrangement was tempting, one of Marilyn's stockings, with the scent of those beautiful thighs over his face. Perhaps just ... 'No, no, I appreciate the offer – but no, I couldn't do that.'

'That a shame, big strong man like you. I think you just give him a few tap with baseball bat, teach him lesson. And I pay you,' she pauses. 'One way or other,' she says with one of her smouldering looks.

Oh God, what was he getting himself into? 'No thanks, I couldn't, nice of you to ask.'

'Okay, but you think about it, you get in touch.'

There was no way Doug was going to get in touch. But getting her out of his thoughts, that was going to be considerably harder. He left Marilyn, saying he was tired and that he thought he'd call it quits for the evening.

Doug had a few qualms about letting himself back

into Charles's place after what had happened. Turning up again got him the odd smirk from people who'd seen Marilyn follow him out.

But where was his wife? He was relieved to see Charles was dancing with Maggie. But no Rachael. He scanned the room mentally checking off the men. Doug apologised to Charles for what had happened earlier in the evening. Charles was very nice about it. He then broke the news about Rachael – she'd taken off home. 'She seemed a tad upset when she noticed what was happening,' said Charles. 'You know, with you and Marilyn.'

Oh God, was he ever in the crap now.

Rachael didn't believe Doug's careful explanation, so things were extremely rocky for several weeks. After a while Doug decided there was something to be said for letting Rachael go on believing he had really had it off with Marilyn. For one thing, she'd given up referring to him as 'careful old Doug'.

As for Charles, well, everything was pretty much as usual, except when they were out of earshot of the others. Then he'd look at Doug in a respectful way: 'You're an old dog, Doug,' he'd say, and give a playful punch on the arm. 'Marilyn … well, I'll be damned. And I thought she was as straightlaced as they come. Never had any success there myself.' His boss had dropped the 'Dougie'.

'Yeah, well …' was all Doug would say.

And once, some weeks later over staff morning tea,

Charles approached with his usual cup of black coffee and gingernut. He stopped in front of Doug, bowed his head slightly, and said in a confidential sort of voice, 'Incidentally, Doug, I've been meaning to ask – where *did* you buy that reefer jacket?'

# The Other Mr Turner

I recently saw the wonderful film *Mr Turner*, with Timothy Spall as William Turner, the early Victorian painter famous for his brilliant skies. It got me remembering another Mr Turner, Mr Ronald Turner.

'Hullo, I'm Mr Turner, Mr Ronald Turner. I live next door, and my wife's name is Mrs Marjory Turner.'

I was a little taken aback by this unusual presentation, a strange introduction to our new neighbours – or rather *we* were the new neighbours, the Turners had lived in the street for fifty-plus years. We were now living in 'the fast lane', or more accurately 'the fast-food lane'. Within a radius of four hundred metres, there were fast-food outlets in almost every direction. McDonalds, California Homestyle Chicken, fish and chips, Pizza Hut and KFC – not the closest but due to the prevailing wind the one we were most conscious of. I had once been fond of KFC, but no longer, with the smell of deep-frying chicken almost constantly hovering around my nostrils.

There was also a video outlet on the corner of our street, and most strategically and appropriately placed on the opposite corner, an undertaker. I imagined the proprietor rubbing his hands at the thought of all the locals getting progressively more obese, sitting glued to their hired videos whilst consuming vast quantities of takeaways. It was only a matter of time. Someone should invent an expanding coffin.

'A pleasure to meet you Mr Ronald Turner,' I said shaking his hand. 'My name is William, but you may as well call me Bill like everyone else.'

'Well then, you can call me Ron.'

'Oh good,' I said.

Ron beamed up at me. I'm not tall, but Ron was very short, and he was deep-chested, nuggety, and really quite old. He looked like he had been in some trade or occupation requiring considerable physical effort. Ron then told me he was retired, as also was Mrs Turner. He said he had run a drycleaning business, which I thought at the time probably accounted for his laboured breathing. I remember the detail of this first encounter as Ron and, to a lesser extent, his wife were to become important characters in the day-to-day drama of our lives.

Our sections were divided by a corrugated-iron fence, with the posts and rails on the Turner side giving Ron somewhere to lean his elbows whilst conversing with me, usually a rather one-sided conversation, which would start almost every time I set foot in our back garden.

'Good day to you, Bill,' Ron would start. What followed was rather difficult to decipher or to translate into anything meaningful, unless you listened very carefully. Ron would ramble on, usually about one of his favourite subjects.

'You'd be way too young to have been in The War, Bill. Me, I was in the New Zealand Div, served in the Middle East and later Italy. Chased Rommel all over the desert – remember Rommel? And when we weren't chasing him, the bastard chased us. Rommel thought us Kiwi soldiers were the best. Supposed to be not a bad bloke himself. Bleeding awful food though … not enough of it. Used to have to wash and shave in one mug of water a day. Didn't go much for the spit-and-polish brigade – intelligence section – bunch of nancy boys … Bloody sand got into everything … eyes, up yer nose, in all your gear. And flies, blimey, even worse than the sand. El Alamein bloody went on night and day … artillery … *boom! Bloody boom! Boom! Bloody boom!* Us infantry jokers had to clean up after the arty … *bang! Bloody bang!* Bayonet charges stuck a few Krauts, poor buggers. Given half a chance we'd rob the bodies of anything valuable – that's war for you.'

On and on he'd go. His presentation was clear enough for starters, but would soon deteriorate into a rumbling mumble. Out of respect for an old soldier, I would have to stop what I was doing and listen carefully so as to get some meaning into what would become a sort of word salad.

I was usually engaged in trying to knock our large back garden into shape – mowing edges, doing a bit of brickwork, putting in a vege garden, painting the shed, making some shingle paths between the planned vegetable beds etc. Stopping to listen to Ron rant on about the war would sometimes make progress jolly near impossible.

Rosie would be watching from the kitchen window. She'd beckon me over. 'Why on earth do you have to stop to listen to that old time-waster when you've got so much to do?'

I could see her point – we'd gone over it many times. Fact is, we'd paid too much for our ninety-year-old cottage, not knowing about values outside the big smoke. We were teetering on the brink of negative equity. It was important to improve the value of the place for when, and if, we ever needed to sell.

Ron had his faults, but he was a great gardener. Vegetables. The whole of their back garden was laid out in immaculate order, an abundance of every type in season. In between World War Two battles he told me about how Invercargill was built on a drained swamp, resulting in beautiful, rich topsoil almost a metre deep. Despite her annoyance at Ron's interference, Rosie soon forgave him when a veritable cornucopia was handed over that iron fence. There's nothing Rosie likes better than fresh veges.

The first peace offering that came our way, which Rosie guessed was to mollify her displeasure at his interruptions, was a very large bunch of rhubarb – enough to feed the whole street. (Actually it was quite a short street.) Being a good Southlander Ron also grew copious quantities of swedes. I hadn't eaten swede since boarding school days, but with the way Marjory instructed us to cook them, they were a delicacy, provided you didn't overdo it. I'll swear I've seen Ron bite into a raw one. I'm told it's not unusual to see Southland farmers eating Swedes like they're very large apples.

Another favourite topic of Ron's was gum digging. That is Kauri gum. I have never before or since met a gum digger.

'It was in the thirties,' said Ron leaning on the fence rail as usual. I'd guessed, later to be confirmed, that Ron stood on a garden seat to reach such a height. He'd seen me digging up the section of lawn where I was going to put in our own vege garden.

'I wasn't much more than a boy, got told the parents couldn't support me anymore, threw me out, hitched my way up north to the gum fields. We were living in Auckland at the time. My dad had got hit pretty hard by the Depression. It was the last time I saw my mum and dad. I missed my mum real bad for years, still do at times. I guess I was angry. I tried to find them when I joined up, but they had moved on. That was the story of my life as a kid, we were always on the move – Dad looking for work.'

Poor old Ron, I felt so sorry for him, but I didn't know how to respond. It made me feel quite bad when

I thought about my own privileged upbringing. I decided then, never to use my 'smarty-pants' tone with Ron. When I told Rosie what he'd said she felt bad as well. Rosie said that's why he'd married Marjory, such a lovely, motherly person.

'On the gum fields,' he went on, 'that's where I learned to use me fists. There weren't many Dallies left at that time. The successful families who had been into Kauri gum from the beginning were off planting vineyards by then. The likes of me were just there for the dregs. Do you know how you do it, Bill?'

'No, to tell you the truth, I've never thought about it.'

'You start with a long steel spike, really long, called a spear, with a handle on one end. You drive the spear down – a lot of swampy land up there, some of it drained ages ago, easier if it's still damp. Yeah, you get the feel for it when you're lucky enough to strike a bit of gum, feels different from a chunk of wood. Then comes the hard part digging down with your spade. If you're lucky it's not a piece of wood, and you've not wasted two or three hours. Most of the good stuff was long gone by the time I got there. Never made me fortune, just enough to feed myself. I set up house in one of the old-timer's abandoned huts. Bloody hard work, Bill – yeah, bloody hard. At least when I got into the army the pay was a lot more regular.

'Sometimes fights broke out over territory in the gum fields. I was good at fighting, came in handy later – always keep your head up otherwise you can't see what's coming at you, and so as you can duck out the way. Yeah, when us infantry jokers were sent in to charge the Jerries with bayonets fixed, you had to keep your wits about so you could see which one had a bead on yah, go for him first before he got you. Pretty gruesome work but, as I say, survived that. Early boxing experience helped. Keep your head up and your eye on the ball.'

He would then get side-tracked into Second Div army life – the highlight being the leave in Cairo, after a particularly hard-fought campaign. But he'd soon be back at the front line.

'Tiny Freyberg was a great boss – looked after us boys … best he could under the circumstances.'

Over time, listening carefully, I learnt quite a lot about the war in the desert.

Beside these interesting bits and pieces about army life and gum digging, and all his other activities and adventures, Ron became a sort of unpaid project manager for whatever job I had currently taken on. At times he had some really good ideas.

'What you up to, Bill?'

I was poking around under the ancient garden shed. It stood about half a metre above ground on some rotten wooden piles, with three steps up to the door,

'I'm thinking of repiling the old shed. Don't fancy working under here, though.'

'If I were you, Bill, I'd know what I'd do.'

'Oh, and what would that be, Ron?'

'It's plain as day to me. It don't need to be perched

so far up off the ground – now does it?'

'No, what's your point?'

'Piece of cake, I was a fireman once, you learn a lot of skills and you learn to use your noddle.'

'So ...?'

I could see he wasn't going to come up with his master plan without a bit of drama.

'Tell you what I'd do if I was you, Bill. First, you've got plenty of space round that shed – every which way. So what you do is this. You plant a new set of concrete piles alongside the old shed – either north or south. The new piles are quite a bit shorter than those old ones. What's the point in having to climb up two or three steps? You fix up some temporary rails and slide the bugger down onto the new piles. Piece of cake. Block and tackle – I've got one somewhere. Attach it to that old apple tree and haul away. Easy as, Bill.'

'My God, you've got something there.' I said. 'Thanks a million.'

Ron was wreathed in smiles as he retreated from his perch – five minutes and he was back with a bunch of the freshest spinach I've ever seen.

'Rosie will be thrilled with this. She makes a great spinach and feta cheese pie.' I make a mental note to suggest Rosie makes one for Ron and Marjory, hoping Rosie too would see the advantage of moving the shed onto a new set of concrete piles.

Then there was the time Ron found an advertisement in the paper, 'Curved Bricks for Sale'.

'What you doing there, Bill – setting out something?'

'Thinking of two or three brick planting-boxes, high enough so we don't have to bend over quite so much.' This was one project Rosie would thoroughly approve of, not just from the bending aspect, but good solid brick planting boxes would be a 'desirable feature,' and increase the value of the property.

'Bill, get yourself a load of these curved bricks, you can make circular planting boxes, that'll look great.'

'Where did you say the bricks are available from?'

'They've pulled down a big chimney at the old Highlander Condensed Milk factory – out along the road to Riverton – you know it? Curved bricks are great for circular jobs. If you get enough you could put down a circular patio as well. What about outside the shed sitting on its new piles? All that shed needs now is a lick of paint, and a nice patio in front – it'd look great.'

I got the bricks, three great big pallet loads. One thing I enjoy is a bit of bricklaying – bit of the Winston Churchill in me. As well as the satisfaction of seeing a project grow before your eyes, there's that ringing sound as you tap the bricks gently into place with the handle of the trowel …

Problem was, it was mid-winter when I got started. Ron as usual was my self-appointed project manager. I mixed up the first bag of trade mortar in the barrow and started in on the bricks. All that leaning over – you need a strong back for this kind of work. First, the brick has to be dunked in a bucket of water. Then, with brick in hand, get a trowel full of mortar and slap it on what is to be the underside. Next, another half trowel-full on one end. Holding it at a slight upward angle so as to keep the end bit of mortar from sliding off – turn it over quick and down onto the row of already placed bricks. The trouble was the Southland winter climate. The water on the brick had turned to ice before I could get the mortar on. As soon as I troweled it on, it slipped off the icy surface and plopped onto the ground. Try as I might, I couldn't get it to stick long enough to get the brick placed.

There was Ron wheezing away on his side of the fence, with hand-knitted beanie pulled well down over his ears, his large nose and eyes all that was visible. Oh, and his mittened hands holding on. I was reminded of the graffiti we saw all over the place in the 60s and 70s: 'Kilroy was here'. Well, Kilroy-Ron quick as a flash came up with the solution to icy bricks. 'You'll have to boil up a kettle and pour boiling water on each brick before you put the mortar on. Are you sure you want to do this in the middle of winter?'

I roped Rosie in to keep up a continuous supply of boiling water. She says I'm a stubborn bastard, but I suspect she enjoyed being part of the action. Worked like a charm, and in no time a perfect circular planting box took shape. Followed in a few weeks by two more. 'You're a genius Ron,' I said. He went off grinning.

Talk about generous people. Southern hospitality was alive and well. That first day of bricklaying, every-thing was freezing, and after we'd cleaned up, Marjory invited Rosie and I over for afternoon tea.

We sat around the kitchen table, the four of us, eating copious quantities of freshly baked scones with lashing of cream and raspberry jam. How do you repay such kindness? After a while Rosie began to appreciate Ron, despite my insistence I must down tools to listen when he was in full flight. Ron had had a long life, and had experienced many different occupations, and quite a few difficulties. Who could not respect an old soldier who had served four years in the Middle East and Italy before being repatriated with a serious shrapnel wound sustained in the Italian campaign?

There was one area where I disagreed with Ron, not that I let him know. That was his hatred of trees. Trees shed their leaves. Ron would climb his extension ladder to clean leaves out of his gutters. Unfortunately there was a gutter on the western side of his roof, next to the other neighbours who had refused his request to cut down, or even trim the trees on their boundary.

There wasn't room between the Turner's house and the fence to prop up a ladder. So occasionally Ron would clamber onto his roof to clean out a particular piece of guttering. I spotted him up there with a stout rope tied around his chest and under his armpits, the other end secured around the brick chimney.

'Hey, Ron!' I called out. 'You're getting a bit too old for that!'

A few minutes later I was alerted to a scraping noise coming from our side of his roof, followed by some muffled groans. I sped through our gate, through his gate, and along the side of the Turner's house. There was poor Ron dangling from the rope and gasping for air, the extra pressure on his chest squeezing the air out or his already compromised lungs.

I moved the ladder alongside him. By this time Rosie had come running. She guided Ron's feet to the ladder, while I climbed a little way up and hauled on Ron's clothing and the rope to swing his weight across so he was left with his back to the ladder. By now dear old Marjory was on the scene, her apron flying, calling out to Ron to keep calm. She shot inside and phoned III.

First to arrive was the fire brigade. Three muscular young men held Ron while another scaled the ladder and untied the rope from the chimney. Ron was taken to A&E. The X-rays showed four cracked ribs, and he spent a couple of nights in hospital.

Unfortunately my hero, mate and project manager, never quite recovered. He took to his bed for longer and longer spells. Heart failure was diagnosed. I missed seeing Ron leaning over the fence.

Eventually I got a transfer back up north, and Rosie said she'd had enough of Southland winters, so we sold up – as it turned out, to a work colleague. Broke evens. Quite a few people were shown around and some open days were held. Several admired the circular planting boxes, the useful garden shed, and the lovely circular brick sitting-out area in the garden.

We kept in touch with Marjory by mail. Ron's situation became dire, and he died a year after we left.

He wasn't much good at expressing himself in words, but if you stopped and listened carefully you got the gist. As Rosie grew to know him better, she too came to respect Ron. She shed a few tears when we got the news, we both did. Marjory's last letter enclosed a little obituary which appeared in the *Southland Times*.

It described how Ron had won the Military Medal for Bravery. The citation was 'for risking his life rescuing and carrying a wounded soldier to safety under enemy fire'. And there was a photo of none other than General Freyberg pinning the medal on Ron's chest.

# Icarus

A niggling doubt remains as she stands at the rail willing the ferry to get under way. Omens, sacrifices to ancient gods, primitive beliefs, none of these could possibly influence the elements, she knows that, but what happened that afternoon had a very strange feel to it.

Resisting the urge to rush down the ramp, where cars are still loading, Ruth scans the wharf expecting Arthur to appear. The thought fills her with dread. Dread and guilt.

Come on! *Come on!* she urges silently. The ferry is already fifteen minutes late.

The boat gives two loud blasts as it edges away from the quay, the sudden fright of it sends sharp pains shooting into her fingers and toes. The shoreline is rapidly receding, and she can only just see the beach where they sat a little over an hour ago. Poor Arthur –

where is he now? Sobbing, she tries to stifle the sadness, and then a strong desire to laugh.

Anger is rising in her chest now, anger at having been driven to this. There have been other occasions when she's thought of leaving, but now it's happening with no plan in mind. Is it all a stupid mistake – misjudgement on her part? Should she go back and try again? Perhaps there is still a chance he could change? But no, he won't change. Not ever.

The town spreads out along the shore and climbs the lower slopes, houses and buildings a white blur beneath the bare sun-baked hillside. A chill breeze slaps her in the face. She realises how cold she's become.

They rose early that morning and drove to the summit in an open-topped jeep. The cold night air had rushed past, catching her hair. How foolish, she thought, not to have worn a scarf. The headlights searched out the soiled grey, cream and whitewashed houses. She felt a stirring of excitement at the prospect of the early morning adventure to watch the sunrise from the highest point on the island.

It was still quite dark when they parked the jeep and scrambled up a rough track past the dim shape of goats, with thyme and sage bushes brushing her legs. Standing on the highest point, leaning against the tiny white, blue-domed chapel, his bulk heaving, Arthur had intoned lines from Keats:

'Or like stout Cortez, when with eagle eyes
He stared at the Pacific – and all his men

> Look'd at each other with a wild surmise –
> Silent, upon a peak in Darien.'

Far from silent, Arthur had gone on with his usual running commentary. 'That island over there, I'm sure that's Naxos. That will be the direction of the sunrise when it comes. These goats, you can just see them now, they pong rather don't they? I trust that's not putting you off the experience, Ruth.' On and on he rambled …

Ruth felt annoyed by Arthur's nonsense. In a setting like this all she wanted was peace, to stand quietly with her thoughts, and to breathe the warm damp air scented with the tangy smell of goat and wild herbs.

As the darkness slipped away they saw a village far below. It looked quiet and empty. First a man appeared, then a dog wandered along the only street. Arthur said how he wished he was one of those toy-like figures emerging from a doorway. 'Peasants,' he said, 'beginning their day, preparing to go off to vineyards, fields, and olive groves.' And he pontificated about wanting to get his hands into 'that ancient soil'. Ruth knew how pointless it was to remind him it was she who looked after their garden at home. She'd moved several metres away – not that he noticed. The goats were now his only audience.

It had been a stunning sight, the sun coming up behind Naxos. Brilliant spiky shafts of light shooting outward, flaring towards Ruth and Arthur, far across a golden-brown sea. A foreground of gently rolling hills and velvety fields – the backdrop, a soft pink and creamy sky. Ruth was reminded of another island where they'd honeymooned years before. She'd believed in romance back then, had even believed in Arthur. They'd found a bar where they would sit sipping ouzo, watching the sun go down across the bay, the sounds of bouzouki music playing nearby …

Having the use of the jeep, Ruth and Arthur spent the remainder of the morning exploring the unspoiled side of the island, away from the town of Paros. She'd wanted to stop for a drink at a quaint old taverna, but Arthur had dismissed the idea – couldn't she see how seedy that place looked? Then later in the morning, he'd refused when she'd asked him to pull in at a small deserted bay so she could have a swim. He insisted they wait and swim at the beach near their hotel.

Arthur had caught sight of a man plowing with his horse between rows of grape vines. If he was an artist he'd paint that scene, he'd said; and then, that he was reminded of Pieter Bruegel's 'Landscape with the Fall of Icarus', a work Ruth was familiar with, but which he then insisted on describing in minute detail. The ploughman in the foreground, his back to the action, how all that could be seen of Icarus was an ankle and a foot as he plunged head first into the waves. 'Poor old Icarus,' he said with feeling. 'What a lonely way to die. No one to witness his fall. No one saw him drowning, no one came to his rescue.'

Ruth was having a vision of her own – a silvery field

of feathers fluttering to earth ... Arthur winging his way toward the sun ...

And now Ruth is standing on the deck and thinking this must surely be the sea that claimed poor proud Icarus. It is the deepest shade of blue she's ever seen. The wind whips spume off the waves and flings it across the deck. Shivering, she pulls the hood of her jacket over her head, and wraps her arms around her chest. Stupid Arthur. Is there still time to make a life for herself?

Following lunch, Ruth and Arthur walked to the beach near their hotel where they usually spent the afternoon. Ruth has never felt at ease surrounded by a mass of perspiring tourists and well-oiled, bare-breasted women, while Arthur always lies on his stomach in the shallows getting an excellent view of the young sunbathers. He must have imagined she was unaware of what he was up to. Out of the water, he rambled on about lotus eaters, and how the traditional islanders must be shocked by such decadence and self-indulgence, all the while gazing around at the women, and those 'pretty boys', as he calls the good-looking young men.

They were stretched out on the sand dozing, when suddenly a deafening crack catapulted them to a sitting position. Not twenty paces away, lying in the shallows, was a large dun-coloured retriever – legs twitching in its death throes. A stocky, bare-footed man stood beside the dog, his baggy trousers bunched at the waist, held up with a piece of rope. He was holding a rifle in one hand. The man bent down, and with the other hand grasped one of the dog's hind legs. Scowling, and looking neither left nor right, he dragged the now inert body up the beach.

A startled silence settled over the frozen tableau of beach dwellers. Almost simultaneously large black clouds billowed up from the horizon, partially obliterating the sun. The air temperature had dropped several degrees. And then, as if from nowhere, a sudden stiff squall swept along the beach making eddies like miniature whirlwinds, sending towels and clothing tumbling across the sand.

It came to Ruth in a flash: killing the dog was something profound, a sign, a final act. She was shivering, but not from cold or fear this time. She was trembling with excitement. What they had just witnessed was a primitive, cruel and dangerous act, but very real – honest even – despite its brutality. That man had shot the dog following some imperative, regardless of the context. She knew in that instant what she must do.

Ruth plunged into the water hoping to clear her mind, to try to understand what was happening. She swam a few strokes, then stood gazing at her surroundings. Everything appeared to her in stark relief: the headland at the end of the bay, the beach and sunbathers, the clarity of the water. The clouds had dispersed, the sun was now fully out again. She looked for Arthur. He was sitting by himself, still appearing perplexed.

She knew in that instant that for once she must follow her impulses rather than forever be constrained by the rules she'd lived by: the self-sacrifice of wife and mother. But what was that: the sky turning black, the sudden chilly wind, so soon after the killing of the dog? Ruth didn't believe in omens, but she wondered if perhaps she could claim what had happened as her own personal omen, presaging some change, something important about to happen in her life. A new beginning!

'That wind squall,' said Arthur, 'was undoubtedly the spirit of that poor creature. It was sacrificed to some ancient God.'

Ruth wanted to say 'rubbish!' but knew it would be a waste of time. She suggested they return to the hotel, and this time Arthur agreed. They followed smears of blood across the road that fringed the bay. The blood trail passed the taverna where they turned left heading for their hotel. Another fifty paces on and it petered out at a crude shack set back among banana palms.

Arthur was in full flight. 'That killing was a sacrifice to appease the Gods for the sins of those hedonists at the beach. Traditional Greeks are offended by such blatant displays of flesh. Or perhaps the man was trying to atone for his own guilt for watching those bare-breasted women.' On, and on he went, totally obsessed.

But Ruth had noticed the chickens. Their mutilated bodies lay in a patch of blood on the yellow clay yard in front of the shack. Little white feathers wafted back and forth in the dust. She pointed, but Arthur refused to acknowledge the evidence, just went on in the same vein, raving about sacrifices to ancient gods, and about hedonists, lotus eaters and guilt ...

Ruth was becoming increasingly angry at his stubborn refusal to face reality, and his crazy insistence on always over-dramatising every subject. The thin veneer of his erudition filtered every situation, all information, every scene. She had never been able to hold an opinion, or just to view the world through her own eyes. She had had enough. Ruth was determined to stand her ground.

They argued angrily over the killings, first the chickens, then the dog. Arthur, with half-clenched fists, cracked his knuckles.

'You're a philistine!' he cried. 'No imagination, no vision!'

'And you've never listened to anything but your own weird imagination,' said Ruth. 'You never take evidence into account, like those dead chickens. That's why the dog was shot, can't you see that?' Ruth's pent up anger was about to boil over.

Arthur said he was returning to the beach.

Ruth continued on toward the hotel. She could see the brightly painted fishing boats moored in the lee of the headland and, closer in, the ferry was manoeuvring to back into the wharf. A gaggle of excited hotel people were already holding up signs touting for business from the incoming tourists. The proprietor of her hotel was himself about to leave for the wharf, but Ruth managed to persuade him to wait while she hurriedly changed, and packed her small suitcase.

The wind is dropping, the ferry is now three hours out, heading for Piraeus. Ruth draws the hood of her jacket away from her head, and as she does so she spots a silver speck just above the horizon in the direction of the island, which is now well out of sight. Two minutes later it's become a much larger silver object. She hears the drone of twin engines.

The plane flies dangerously low over the ferry, dipping its wings as it passes, also heading in the direction of Piraeus.

The very correct and sympathetic police inspector finds Ruth in a pension on Corfu. He is most apologetic as he explains how a light plane crashed into the sea just off Piraeus, killing the pilot and only passenger. Insufficient fuel it seems. They left in a great hurry according to witnesses. No one actually saw the crash. The evidence points to the passenger being her husband, and would she please proceed to Piraeus to formally identify the body.

# Coach

On a visit back to Wellington, without realising it, Morris finds himself in Marion Street; the hangout for a bunch of hard case 'working girls' back in the day. It's now a place of shops, upmarket apartments and offices. All that remains of the girls he remembers is a painting of one of them on the corner building where Marion intersects with Ghuznee Street. Standing looking at the mural, Morris is flooded with memories of one night, fifteen years ago – probably longer.

'Care to join me,' Daphne throws back the duvet.

Morris nearly drops the cup of tea he's delivering. 'No thanks, I'm watching the game.'

Daphne grimaces and flings herself over to face the wall. She's just woken from her customary afternoon weekend nap.

If she thinks she can get me to do that on demand!

thinks Morris. Not like Daph, though, flaunting herself. I bet she's been dreaming about her new boss at the library. Librarians tend to look down on us mere mortals. He'd overheard her describing the boss to her friends as an intellectual who took great care with his appearance. Sleek-looking, she'd said, adding with a sigh, 'If only I was several years younger.'

Several years and the rest. Daph will be safe as houses with *him*, thinks Morris. And anyway, he's probably gay.

She couldn't really want it, just her way of making Morris feel inadequate. That, and the put-downs about accepting a very inadequate redundancy pay-out from Her Majesty's Customs Service. The way she talks you'd think she's always been the sole breadwinner.

That evening they drive in to see a film. Her choice again, always the same, some art movie or a foreigner with sub-titles, a lot of talk and romantic stuff with bugger-all action.

Afterwards, they're walking back to the car. It's dark. While they've been in the cinema the town has come to life. Cafés, bars and restaurants are all lit up. The streets are full of young people looking for a good time, dressed-up, made-up, heading for a bar, or hoping for an encounter.

Morris is covertly letting Daphne lead the way. This is not the first time he's been unable to remember where they've parked. As he glances sideways at her, he's wondering again whether she really wanted him to do the business this afternoon. Something in that film has stirred him up a little. He spots the car – of course he knew it was right there, up the top of Ghuznee Street.

But when Morris tries to start her, there's not even a whimper.

'Daphne, you forgot to turn off the lights, didn't you? You were the one who drove in.'

'Rubbish, you were driving and you must have left the lights on,' says Daphne with conviction.

She sometimes drives when Morris has been to the rugby club; not that he drinks much, it's merely a precaution. He wasn't at the club that afternoon, but it was worth a try.

'I could swear it was you, and you've got to admit you're a little champ when it comes to leaving things switched on.'

'Were you at the rugby club this afternoon? No, you weren't,' says Daphne.

There she goes again, always scoring points, always the moral high ground.

'Well, you should have checked,' says Morris. 'I'm expected to do every goddamned thing. Okay, okay, you steer and I'll push. Stick her in gear, and when she gets a bit of momentum let in the clutch. And for God's sake keep her running as soon as she fires. And watch out at the intersections, it's hellish busy out there. Saturday night!'

Morris starts pushing the Mitsubishi down Ghuznee Street.

'Want a hand?'

'Yeah thanks, I'd appreciate it.'

The young man is quite skinny, but the way he puts his hands on the boot and starts to push shows he can do his share of the work.

'I'm getting a bit old for this caper,' puffs Morris. 'Not as fit as I was at your age, young fellah. Would you believe I once played rugby for Petone. Tighthead prop. How about you? You into any sport?'

'No, not really.'

Two or three attempts at engaging the clutch have produced nothing. They have negotiated the Victoria Street lights, but only just … a really scary business. They're now approaching the Cuba Street intersection.

'D'yer think she's got it switched on?' says the young man.

'Good point. Hey, Daph!' She hates him calling her Daph. 'Hold her a sec!' Morris is moving round beside the driver's door and signing for her to lower the window. 'Just as I thought – you haven't got it switched on. For crying out loud!'

'You didn't tell me to switch it on. All you said was put it in gear and let the clutch in when it's moving.'

'You could have used a bit of common … Let's have another go. Quick now the lights are green, we'll get across Cuba Street …' He makes his way back around the car. 'Blimmin woman,' he mutters, out of Daph's earshot, rolling his eyes at his phlegmatic young helper.

They're moving forward again, but half way across the intersection Daphne stands on the brakes. At the back, it's as if they've hit the entire All Black tight five. Morris raises his head to yell at Daphne, 'Hey!' But the curse dies on his lips as he spots a couple of gang members strolling across the road in front of the car. Is that the Black Power salute, or are we getting the fingers? His head isn't up long enough to sort out which.

They are safely across the intersection when the young man makes a suggestion. 'We're not doing too well are we? How about we turn into Marion Street? If we push her up and turn at the top we'll have a good clear run back down. Marion's got a bit of a slope to it.' He's quite serious, thinks Morris, could easily be a final year varsity student, or maybe an adult apprentice – electrical, or plumbing. Not much of a sense of humour though.

The information about Marion having a slope is news to Morris, but he isn't going to argue the point with his young benefactor. 'Hey, Daphne, swing into Marion Street, but for God's sake watch out for traffic coming the other way!'

That's when the titillation begins. Morris has entirely forgotten Marion Street is the working girls' favourite haunt. The first one they encounter is wearing leather lace-up boots with black satin hot pants. Up top is a low-slung, knitted, sleeveless thing – iridescent green, Morris thinks, but she's half in shadow so he's not sure.

'Ooh, there's a couple of cute little bums. Put a bit of grunt into it, my darlings. I can see you two screwing the scrum, yeah, all eight of them.' It is a suspiciously deep throaty voice.

A little further up, on the opposite side of the street, a squat woman is standing on the corner of an alley. She's striking a pose with stubby legs apart and a thrusting pelvis, hands on hips. 'You guys are pretty good at pushing and heaving. Step this way, gents, and give me a piece of the action. I'll take the young one first, he'll be real quick about it, guarantee.' Followed by a burst of raucous laughter.

Morris is relieved to recognise a genuine female voice. Others are joining in the merry chorus as they progress up the street.

'Hello sailors, don't waste all your energy on that old bomb!'

'I could show you a thing or two about pushing, my darlings.'

'How about a blow job without the puff job – he he he!'

Gales of laughter up and down the street.

Morris relished a little light banter himself, but not this evening, not with Daphne in the driving seat. And besides, he's gasping for air. Daphne's window is wound right up, and he wonders how many of the ribald comments she's taking in. She'll be disgusted with the vulgarity.

They reach the top of Marion Street, at which point he instructs Daphne to hold the wheel hard over. They manage to swing her round in one, and with the young man's help Morris puts in a last mighty effort. The cheerleaders continue their good-natured encouragement all the way back down the street.

Still she fails to fire. There is nothing for it but to roll her into the kerb down by the corner. The young man shakes his head, says something about it needing more than a push.

'Thanks, young fellah, you should take up rugby.' Morris offers him five dollars for a beer.

'Nah, it's nothing, thanks all the same.' He does up his jacket and straightens his tie. 'Must be off, got a date.'

Typical generous spirit of the male of the species, thinks Morris, as his friend disappears round the corner.

And then: 'Jump leads,' he says. 'Jump leads, I'll get hold of a pair of jumper leads.' He would now have to fathom this on his own.

'And where do you propose getting jumper leads at this hour?' says Daphne reminding him of her somewhat unnerving presence. She's rolled down the car window and is leaning out.

I'm going to be blamed for this whole sequence of events, thinks Morris. 'I'll just duck up to Abel Smith Street, there's an all-night garage up there, they'll lend me some, or they might even come to the rescue.'

Off he goes at a brisk walk, every now and then breaking into a measured jog, temporarily forgetting that Daphne is sitting not five paces from the trannie with the deep voice.

It is quite exhilarating being out in the night air away from Daphne's gaze, but it's beginning to dawn on him that Abel Smith Street is a lot further away than he remembered. By the time he arrives he's dripping perspiration. A new building occupies the site where the all-nighter had previously stood. He's getting worried about Daphne, imagining her getting crosser by the minute.

Morris remembers seeing a service station in Vivian Street. Off he trots, making resolutions about getting into shape. He thinks of the old chap he saw a couple of days earlier, rollerblading along the foreshore. Yes, Morris thinks, he'll give that a go. Gliding at speed, creating his own slipstream, young women giving him admiring glances. He spots the Shell garage just round the corner from Cuba Street. It's all lit up and looks welcoming.

'I'm wondering … ah … if I could borrow some jump leads. I'm down in Marion Street … got a flat battery …'

'Sorry Sir, we don't have any leads to lend out.' The attendant is polite, but he is eyeing Morris suspiciously.

Just because I'm stuck in Marion Street, thinks Morris, he reckons I must be one of those sleazy kerb-crawler jokers.

'What do you suggest? Got any ideas, mate?'

'Just a sec. See that cabbie over there? Yeah, the woman filling up the white Toyota Crown, she usually carries a set of leads.'

'Thanks, mate.' It would have to be a woman, and she looks like a scary old dragon.

'Excuse me, the boss says you've got some jumper leads. I wonder if it's possible to borrow them. I'm down in Marion Street with a flat battery.'

'Marion, eh?' She too looks at Morris with half-closed eyes. 'Yeah, I've got some leads.' She opens the boot of the Toyota. 'Well I'll be buggered! Those little scrotes! I took some kids to the railway station this morning. I opened the boot from the inside so they could get their gear out ... those little *scrotes* must have pinched me jump leads. Wait till I get my hands on them. Hang on, I'll see if I can borrow some.' She slams the boot so hard it makes Morris wince.

'The man I spoke to said they didn't have any.'

'Just you wait there, it's not what you know, it's who yer knows.' She is back in sixty seconds with a set of leads. 'Hop in, I'll run yer down.'

The woman continues her tirade against 'those little scrotes' all the way to Marion Street, repeating the same line over and over till Morris is ready to strangle her with the leads. Typical bloody woman: Talk, talk, talk, never let up.

'Just round the corner,' says Morris. 'The Mitsubishi there under the street light.'

Demonstrating considerable skill, the cabbie man-oeuvres alongside.

Daphne isn't there. She must have taken off somewhere, gone for a stroll. Silly woman! Doesn't she know how dangerous it is this time of night? They connect up and the car roars to life. As Morris hoped, it's a flat battery. He keeps her running with a foot on the accelerator while fishing around for his wallet to pay the cabbie. With that accomplished, Morris focuses his mind on Daphne's whereabouts.

'Welcome back, sailor. Care for a good time?' The tall one with the deep voice emerges from the shadows. 'What about a quickie, hand or blow-job, what's your preference?'

Morris takes a couple of steps backward almost falling over the kerb. He's relieved to have a legitimate reason to change the subject. 'Did you see my wife, she was sitting in the car right there?'

'Yes, dear heart, I saw her. Indeed I did. Just a few minutes ago I suggested she go round the corner for a nice cup of coffee. She said she was fed up waiting for you, Big Boy. And I'll bet you are a big boy too. You're one of the regulars round here aren't you?'

'Wha…? That'll be the day! And you can cut that out.'

'I'm sure I know you from somewhere. D'you live in Petone?'

'Yes.' Morris is getting worried about this familiarity thing. It's a relief Daphne isn't around to hear it.

'I know, I remember you. You used to coach kids' rugby, didn't you?'

'Well, yeah, I did as a matter of fact. Several years ago.'

'Do you remember the lanky kid in your team who used to play on the side of the scrum? My name was Jason then, I'm Jacinta now. Nice name don't you think, Coach? You used to say I showed real promise … ooh fancy that! What I liked best though, Coach, was when you'd tell me to pack down lower in the scrum, and you'd give me a little pat on the bottom. He! He! Ooh, I loved that. We've still got time for a quickie.

Just down the alley there, Coach, behind that little sheddy thing.'

'No thank you!' Morris gets into the car, winds up the window and locks the doors. So begins the longest twenty minutes of his entire fifty-eight years. He starts the engine and keeps it running, revving it from time to time.

Finally Daphne appears round the corner. Phew! Morris is relieved to see his wife's confident, familiar face and shape. Seeing her under the street light, he thinks to himself that she's really quite nice-looking for a woman of her age, not a bad figure either.

It's 11.15pm and they can finally head for home. Morris is still feeling shaken.

'What have you been up to?' he says, 'I've been waiting ages.'

'You've been waiting for *me!* That must have been at least three-quarters of an hour I'd been sitting there, while you were off looking for your blessed jumper leads.'

'Sorry to have been so long,' he says. 'As a matter of fact I was getting worried about you stuck there amongst all these pros.'

'That part was all right, actually, it was a bit of an education. But, as for the men driving round and round the block eyeing the women up. Disgusting!'

'Kerb-crawlers, they're called kerb-crawlers.'

'How do you know about such things?'

'Everyone knows about such things. Everyone except you, Daphne.'

'Well it was a bit disconcerting, one of them kept

staring at me every time he drove past, d'you think he thought I was, you know, one of them?'

'I doubt it, not at your age, probably worried you looked like his mother.' Morris enjoys that little thrust. 'Pretty disgusting those girls yelling out that stuff while we were pushing the car, don't you think. Could you hear what they were saying?'

'Oh, I thought they were most amusing, calling you names, and giving you those funny invitations.'

'I didn't think it was that funny,' says Morris.

'It's awful though, what they have to do, selling themselves to make a living. And those creepy crawlers looking them over like they're at a cattle sale. You men have got a lot to answer for.'

'Here we go again. So it's men getting the blame is it? Like with everything else, us men are to blame.'

'The women are probably very nice people who've got children at home to support,' says Daphne. 'As a matter of fact I had a chat with one of them, the tall dark one heavily made up with the deep voice, next to where I was sitting. She was very kind. I'd been there quite a while when she came over to ask if I was all right, and whether you'd taken off and left me. She said if I wanted to go round the corner for a coffee, she'd keep an eye on the car. And you too if you came back. That was nice of her, wasn't it?'

'I don't know about that, Daphne. Can't we get off this subject?'

All this talk was stirring up Morris' discomfort. That

Jason saying he'd patted his arse. I never did any such thing, thinks Morris. I'm sure I never did … he was just trying to wind me up. But the thought of it is still making him feel peculiar. It has completely spoiled the entire evening.

'Anyway, I thought it was a very interesting experience.'

'Yeah, Daphne, you have it your own way.'

Later that same evening Morris makes a Milo for them both. As he sits sipping his drink he thinks about that team of twelve-year-olds he coached, the one with Jason in it. Of course, he realises now, his son Scott was in the same team. They'd done really well, top of the table in their grade. He'd been so proud of that team. They really put their all into winning, and he knew his coaching had a lot to do with their success.

Evenings under floodlights, the cold night air, condensation on the breath, wet grass underfoot. The sheer exhilaration of it all. It was one of the best experiences of his life. I could take it up again, he thinks.

Morris continued coaching kids' rugby until he needed the second hip replacement, and he's come down to Petone now to celebrate a milestone in the club's history. They moved to Auckland to be near Scott and his wife and the grandchildren. They rent a small apartment on the North Shore. Daphne fills in at the local library whenever they are short-handed.

It's funny being back in Wellington on his own. With time on his hands, Morris has taken the bus into

Wellington. He's enjoying strolling around the city, noticing some of the changes that have occurred, when he finds himself back on Marion Street.

# A Grey Area

The body's been found.

Mid-winter and everything's grey; different layers and shades of grey. The lake's a shiny steely grey; frequent squalls driven by a mean sou'west wind are corrugating the surface. I can just make out the distant mountains. They'll be completely covered in snow at this time of year, but with the sun almost hidden behind cloud, they too look grey.

The town's behind me, this town I've come to despise.

I walk this way every lunch hour, but today I'm spending longer staring across the lake, which only hours ago gave up his body. There's a lot to think about but I'm surprised how calm I feel, more on top of things than I've felt for quite some time.

Boats in the middle distance look like midges fallen into a thin grey soup. The small number of fishing boats I can see are keeping close in shore. Sensible, not like McKenna.

The news report said he was wearing a life jacket, but that he couldn't have survived long in the very cold water at this time of year. His boat washed up some twenty-four hours earlier. They said there was no sign of a bung, and the bailer was missing. Both were found in his garage. Is that strange? Not really, it could happen to anyone as impatient and careless as McKenna.

The police interviewed me the day before yesterday along with other members of the committee, probably the last group of people to have seen him alive. Just routine, they said. I told them how he'd announced his fishing trip at the end of the meeting. 'I'll be off real early,' he'd said. 'You folks'll still be snoring.' And when we declined the invitation to accompany him, it was, 'All the more for me, and I suppose you bludgers'll be expecting a share of the catch. Fat chance!'

The wind's getting up, the surface of the lake's quite choppy, but nothing compared to last Saturday when McKenna failed to return.

What I didn't mention to the police, didn't think it necessary, was the way he'd made it his life's mission to make me as miserable as he possibly could.

When the bank transferred us here eighteen months ago, I volunteered to be treasurer of the Lions Club, taking over the job from my predecessor. Community service is expected of managers.

To my horror, I discovered the club chairman was

none other than Frank McKenna. When I addressed the chair to make a point, he'd stare at me with those dead-fish eyes, 'So, the Invisible Man wants to speak?' The Invisible Man is the name McKenna coined for me so long ago. I've heard it hundreds of times over the years.

At last Friday's meeting, he took great delight in telling the committee how I'd fainted the previous day. I'd given my pint of blood at the donor service and was sitting recovering with a cup of tea and biscuit, when down I went. I came round with this grotesque figure looming over me. 'Well I'll be buggered, if it's not you, Invisible Man! What in God's name are you doing down there, you pathetic little sod?'

Just one more insult heaped on top of all the others. I was surprised he was a blood donor, though – there had to be some political mileage in it for McKenna to part with his blood. But then he made no secret of his ambition to one day enter Parliament. Heaven help the poor and dispossessed if he'd lived to attain that goal.

I'm wondering if any other member of the committee mentioned this blood donor thing to the police, and his constant attacks on me. No reason for them to make anything of it, he was well known around town for his arrogance and bad manners. How he made such a success of his vehicle franchise remains a mystery. There's no doubt McKenna was wealthy. He was forever using his position on the committee to feather his own nest – service to the community was not a concept he understood. He and I argued over that. But McKenna was skilled with words. He used them like cudgels, which usually got him what he wanted.

We went back a long way.

In two of our primary school photos all you can see is the top of my head; the photographer can't have noticed I was even there. If he had, he'd have hauled me into the front row with the other small kids. McKenna is standing there in the back row larger than the others, arms folded across his chest, a big loud, energetic – probably hyperactive – bully of a kid. That name he gave me caught on, even some of the teachers called me Invisible Man. I guess the label fitted. I was small, pale and timid. Desperately wanting to be included in games, I'd hang around the sidelines, but when I tried to join in McKenna would say something like, 'Nah, piss off, we don't want that little runt playing with us.'

Standing here looking at the lake that silenced him, I'm saddened at the thought of all I missed as a child because of that man. The sou'wester's blowing off the lake with greater intensity now. I button my coat up to the neck, vaguely aware of rubbish and fallen leaves gusting around my ankles.

When we moved on to secondary school, McKenna was still around, larger and louder than ever, the sort of leader other kids followed out of fear rather than respect. Come the winter it was, 'So the Invisible Man's not playing rugby this year, probably playing netball, if the girls will let him – the little poof.' And in class it would be, 'Watch out for the Invisible Man, he cheats – you can't see him looking over yah shoulder copying yah work cos he's invisible – ha ha!' This was a neat projection on Frank's part, teachers had caught him cheating on several occasions. It was an early indicator as to how he'd get ahead in life, stealing ideas and blaming others.

When I did my compulsory military training, he became a sergeant, and – by some cruel quirk of fate – was transferred to my platoon. Sergeant McKenna was loud, ruthless, and dishonest. 'Private Invisible, there's dirt down yah barrel – take a look for yerself!'

I'd go through the motions of peering down my rifle barrel knowing full well it was spotless. 'Private Invisible, that's a greasy mark on yah battle dress,' as he wiped an oily finger from the breach of his own rifle across my tunic. 'You're on a charge. Report to me at 1700 hours with yah rifle and full kit!'

I'd be given extra drill at the double, with McKenna screaming contradictory orders across the bullring.

The police don't need to know any of this. I haven't told anyone, not even my wife knows. I guess at one level I've felt ashamed. He got me believing I was some sort of freak, like that battered wives' syndrome we hear about.

I remove my hat and turn to face the freezing wind. I often do this; it's part of a process I started several months ago to toughen myself both physically and mentally. Survival training I call it. I won't be giving it up either, at least not for a while.

There's another thing I omitted telling the police. That's how McKenna would leave his garage door rolled up overnight, before going off on one of his early morning fishing expeditions. The streetlight shone on his flash BMW, and of course the boat he was so proud of. As well as showing off the baubles of his success, the open garage door allowed for a quick getaway in the morning. Typical of the man – always in a rush. Anyway, everyone knows how impatient and careless McKenna was, how he'd speed out into the middle of the lake regardless of weather reports and the warnings of more experienced fishermen. There'd be little time given to checking his gear. I often pass that way when I'm taking the dog for his nightly walk.

Following the accident, the police warned boaties on the radio to always check their equipment. Spare petrol, a bailer *tied on* – they emphasised that – and to make quite certain the bung was securely fixed into the boat.

Far out on the lake it's raining. A wide shaft of brownish-grey rain joins lake and sky together. It appears as if it's going upwards into the cloud, and not vice versa; I guess the light's playing tricks. Then again, things are not always as they appear.

I'd better get back to the bank. It'll be more of the same, listening to the local businessmen complaining how quiet things are at this time of year. I've come to loathe this town and everyone in it, but right now I'm feeling quite light-hearted. It's strange. I'm feeling nothing else really, nothing else at all.

I'll suggest some flowers from the committee.

Anyone passing at this moment could easily overlook a small man gazing south across the lake, wearing a grey overcoat, with a grey felt hat pulled well down over his eyes. They'd probably be intent on watching the rainbow arching across the lake. It's just the sort of weather for rainbows.

# Northbound All the Way

'Wonderful!' I said it aloud.

I'd just come from a meeting with my sister and brother-in-law. The outcome: they would buy out my half share of the family farm we'd inherited. They'd even come up with a substantial deposit – the balance to be paid off over the next few years.

I was still feeling thoroughly elated when I boarded the northbound train. Inhaling a musky perfume, I hitched my briefcase into the overhead rack. A young woman sat facing me wearing a cream raincoat, unbuttoned, and beneath that a navy suit with short close-fitting skirt. She was looking out the window, but I noticed her giving me a sidelong glance. When she turned toward me in response to my greeting, I saw a face with character, the features not particularly symmetrical, but undeniably sexy.

Her left eye turned outward ever so slightly – I'm still

not sure why I found this so attractive. Both eyes were a deep, deep shade of blue, accentuated by a significant dilation of the pupils. She had a beautiful mouth, fully developed with the upper lip deeper at the centre, which gave it a wonderfully sensuous appearance.

Finding her presence unsettling I was relieved to have my notepad handy. I began some desultory jottings.

'Do you often travel on this train?' she said.

'Not frequently, unfortunately. What I mean by that is I like travelling by train, not having the strain of driving, and I like its predictability. I guess it suits my … ah, the way I am. And you?'

'When I visit my parents, which isn't often.'

'So, is that where you're going now?'

'No no, I've just been – what a waste of time. I'd been hoping my dad could help out with my finances.'

Following these snatches of self-revelation, the conversation lapsed into an embarrassed silence. I returned to my scribbling, but was having difficulty. With my head down I was distracted by the young woman's lovely legs, which were bare despite the early spring weather.

I experienced a flush of excitement when finally she spoke again. 'Are you a writer?'

'Actually I'm a consultant. Hospital administration is my field, but yes I do a little scribbling in my spare time. For some reason I'm having trouble finishing this particular story.'

'What are you writing about?'

'It's a love story. I sometimes write for one of the women's magazines. They've asked me to beef this one up with a little erotic content. I suspect they're trying to boost a flagging circulation.' I grinned nervously, thinking she may consider me something of a weirdo. But she returned my smile and I noticed her looking at me in an unusually attentive way, which I found flattering.

'How extraordinary!' she said, 'I'm a student of English doing a Master's. The subject I'm researching happens to be the erotic content in nineteenth century English novels. Now there's a coincidence. So you're having trouble with the way this one's shaping up?'

'Yes, it's difficult. I'll admit I'm confused about some of it. When I read the words I've written they evoke in me certain feelings all right, but the particular situation I've written about is based on my own experience.' I considered this exaggeration excusable under the circumstances. 'The thing is, are the words themselves sufficiently imbued with common meanings to convey an erotic flavour to the average reader? What I'm not sure about is whether it's the words that are resonating, or is it simply my memories of certain situations that make the story work. It's hard to be objective, isn't it? Am I boring you?'

'Not at all, I can appreciate the dilemma. Some of the stuff I plough through in my reading is supposed to be erotic, or that must have been the author's intention, but frankly a lot of it leaves me cold.' She continued, 'Do you *hear* the words you are writing, or do you just see them on the page?'

'Definitely hear them. I'm predominantly an auditory person.' While I was saying this I was thinking about her voice. It was an educated middle-class voice with a lovely rich lilt to it. Those deep blue eyes were expressive, and they sparkled as she spoke appearing to mirror the lilt in her voice. She held my gaze as if issuing a challenge. Or she could have been mocking me.

'I've been playing around with words for this story far more than I usually do,' I said.

'Perhaps you'd like to explore some erotic words with me, see what we could come up with?'

It sounded risky but having set off in this direction I was already half committed, and besides, she probably knew more about the subject than I did. I might learn something. 'Thanks, I'd appreciate that.'

'We could take turns. Can I suggest we start with some fairly neutral words, and work toward ones that are more erotically charged.' I was watching her face as she spoke. She wore the faintest trace of lipstick, which complemented the sensuousness of her mouth. When she listened it was with lips slightly parted.

'I'll start,' she said, 'What about *tempt?*'

'As opposed to, say, *provoke* or *entice?*' I said. 'I think entice may have it over tempt – but they're about even in my book.'

'Yes I can agree with that. Your turn. Incidentally, how far are you going? This may take a while.'

'Right through. What about you?'

'I'm going all the way too, so that's all right.' I caught the double entendre as she proffered her hand. 'By the way my name's Leonie.'

'I'm Alex.' I searched her eyes again as we clasped hands. Hers felt cool and the handshake firm, but then her hand relaxed and lingered in my grasp longer than I'd have expected.

Looking back now, I'm pretty sure Leonie had already settled on her own agenda. I've questioned my motives too. I may well have fleetingly considered it more than an academic exercise, but since my wife left me I'm usually committed to proceeding with caution where women are concerned.

'*Raunchy*,' I said, then felt foolish.

'Ah, well, you're leaping ahead. But it's a good one, depending on the flavour of the piece.'

I began to relax. '*Rapacious*,' I said, forgetting it was Leonie's turn. 'I don't like it, though – it has overtones of nastiness. We'll discard that one shall we?'

'Suits me. My turn,' said Leonie. 'Let's think … *fervent*. It's a favourite of those nineteenth century novelists. Hasn't got much guts to it though.'

'What about *eager*,' I said. 'Has a sense of urgency about it.'

'Yes, I like *eager*; it could be used where clothing's being ripped off.' As Leonie said this, I was certain her eyes travelled down my shirt front.

'*Sensuous* has a full-bodied sound to it.'

'Yes, that's a good one. My turn. How about *sordid?* I think I have a problem with that, though. I know sex can be exploitative, but I like to think of it as connected with fun. *Sordid* is hardly a fun word, or even erotic for that matter.' If I'd known what was to follow I may have had second thoughts about that subject.

We carried on in this vein going through a number of possibilities: *passion, ecstasy, blushing, throbbing, heaving, quivering, swelling, breathless, fiery* … and several others.

'*Attract … attractive* … what do you think?' she said.

I was becoming increasingly excited. And I could have misinterpreted the signs, but I was sure her pupils had dilated more since we'd begun our exercise. Her nostrils were flaring slightly, and those lovely lips were parted further. I was conscious of a tightness around my thighs, and I could feel my diaphragm contracting.

It was my turn. '*Attract* has to be a useful word, a forerunner to flirtation, or even seduction.' The ease with which I was saying these words surprised me. *Smouldering* is the word that comes closest to describing the look she gave me. I began feeling anxious again.

'*Seduction* is a loaded word,' said Leonie. 'A full-bodied fleshy sort of word.'

I nodded in agreement. My breathing had become shallow making it difficult to pronounce the words. '*Yearning, longing* …' I managed, 'Which do you prefer?'

'I like *longing*, it's fuller, more voluptuous. *Yearning* is okay, but I prefer longing.' Her voice trailed off with these last words. I felt the pressure of her calf against my own. She'd slid forward in the seat extending her legs which were now parted, stretching her tight little skirt. My heart was racing and my whole body was infused with desire – a delicious, tender longing.

As if reading my mood Leonie said a little breathlessly, '*Desire*, yes, desire has some fire to it.' It wasn't so much what she was saying, it was the way her beautiful, sexy lips mouthed the words. I knew all about desire at that moment. I was trembling, and she would have been able to feel that where our legs were locked together. Leonie was fondling her lower lip with pale, strong-looking fingers. I could see the tip of her tongue which she began caressing, very gently.

I desperately searched for a neutral word to bring us back from the brink. '*Concupiscence.*'

'*Concu*–what? What does that mean? I've never heard of it.'

'It means lust or sexual desire.' I felt deflated by the strength of her reaction.

'It has a very clinical sound to it,' she said, raising her eyebrows and looking peeved. 'Why not use those much earthier ones – lust or even sexual desire.'

'You're quite right, familiar words are often more effective than obscure ones.' God, how trite that sounded. There's no doubt she was more in control of the situation than I at that particular moment.

'*Willing*,' said Leonie. 'I like that word, what do you think?' There was no mistaking her meaning.

How am I going to handle this situation? I thought. My heart was pumping like mad. But I knew then I wasn't going to let this opportunity go, despite my anxiety. 'Sure,' I said. 'I'm willing, more than willing, if you are, but I don't see what we can do about it right here on the train.' I was experiencing a strong sexual tension throughout my entire body.

Leonie had an idea. 'There's a toilet at the end of this carriage. Are you still willing?' She must have sensed my anxiety. I nodded, in the state I was in anywhere would have done.

'Let's go then. We'll look like we're heading for the dining car and just dive in there.' She stood up and removed her raincoat and navy suit jacket, placing them in the luggage rack. The cream, close-fitting blouse showed off her small firm breasts.

Something about safe sex crossed my mind. 'I haven't got anything.'

'That's all right, don't worry.' She grasped my arm looking me straight in the eye. We bundled into the toilet. 'No one saw us – quick lock the door.'

Straight away we were at each other. I was trembling all over now, feeling like a sixteen-year-old, and quite oblivious to our surroundings. My fingers weren't functioning properly; I needed help to unbutton her blouse. I caught my breath. Her bra was a delicate shade of pink, trimmed with white lace. I slipped my left hand inside it and began gently stroking her right breast moving outward to the erect nipple, tweaking it between my thumb and forefinger. Leonie slipped the bra strap off her shoulder giving me total access.

My right hand pulled up her skirt as she unbuckled my belt and dropped my trousers. I backed her up against the small hand-basin which was just the right height to support the curve of her delightful little bottom. She was stroking my inner thigh and buttocks. I could feel wetness through the crotch of her pants. She was gasping as I began caressing the smooth flesh, which opened to the movement of my hand, causing her to shudder. God, I thought, she's going to climax already.

The way things were shaping, there'd be no need for protracted foreplay. Leonie pulled my head down and our mouths meshed in an extraordinarily erotic kiss. My mind was racing ahead anticipating what was to come, and calculating I'd have no trouble entering her via the leg of her silky French panties.

That's when Leonie tensed.

'No! No, no, *no!* This isn't right – and we shouldn't be doing it without a condom. Stop right there! I'm sorry, Alex.'

My hand was still on the silky crotch of her pants, but she was sliding away now and adjusting her skirt. Utterly confounded, I bent down and pulled up my trousers. Leonie buttoned her blouse and smoothed her hair. She appeared to have regained her composure, while I remained shaking at the knees, hardly able to stand.

We were out of there almost immediately. Leonie led the way as we headed for the dining car.

'Where are you staying tonight?' I asked, my heart thumping furiously as we seated ourselves.

'Where I live, of course – with my flatmate.'

'Can I see you again?'

'Look, Alex, I don't think that's a good idea.'

'What, what's wrong, was there something – ?'

'No, it's nothing like that. Don't look so hurt. There's something I've got to do, and I need to be single-minded about it, for a while anyway … well, I really don't know for how long.' She placed a hand over mine in a reassuring gesture.

'I don't understand, what's all this about?'

'I suppose I should tell you, but it's difficult. You see, Alex, you've been used in a sort of experiment. Oh God, I hate having to say this. It's something I needed to find out for myself, and I'm very sorry I had to involve you. I picked the wrong guy, you're really very sweet.'

I withdrew my hand. 'The wrong guy! An experiment! What do you mean, an *experiment*?'

The other diners would have heard every word of this last sentence.

'I guess I should tell you. It's to do with my horribly large student loan. It's weighing me down. That level of debt is really frightening, and now my dad can't help, he was my last hope, I've decided to become a "working girl" till I can get the debt down to where I can sleep at night. I hate having to tell you this.'

'You must be desperate. But where in God's name did I come into your plans?'

'I'm sorry, you just happened to be available at the time when I needed to find out whether or not I could do it with a complete stranger. I'm not usually into one-off sex, have never considered myself particularly promiscuous, and I had to find out if I could go through with it. That's all there is to it.'

'You found out you couldn't, that's why we stopped.'

'No, on the contrary I could have so easily gone ahead.'

I'd been so excited by this young woman, and now ... 'For God's sake! You've surely messed around with my emotions – I'm absolutely shattered. Can you understand that?'

We sat out the remainder of the journey, only a further thirty minutes as it happened, with hardly a word passing between us. She left the carriage ahead of me. In such a short acquaintance I'd become hopelessly infatuated; attracted to her mind as well as her body. And now it was over. All that remained of Leonie was the back of her lovely head rapidly disappearing down the platform.

A possibility suddenly came to me, it was surprising it hadn't occurred to me earlier. I sprinted, catching her up at the entrance to the concourse.

'Wait, wait, Leonie, can we talk?'

It's been eighteen months now and her loan must be close to being paid off. So far she hasn't mentioned, and I haven't had the courage to ask, what will happen when that day arrives.

# The Wedding Cake

How could he forget when the previous evening he'd been reminded on no less than three occasions, and, in front of all those people. They'd been down at the hall arranging the flowers, trestle tables, seating, crockery, glassware, cutlery, and a hundred and one things that needed doing. Patsy had been in her element. Having assembled several friends and family members, she'd proceeded to do almost everything herself. Firing off instructions, countermanding them, whilst stuffing assorted vases and jars with quantities of delphiniums, jonquils, roses, daisies, hydrangeas, assorted lilies, such a lot of flowers she'd managed to wheedle out of everyone.

The helpers kept hearing how much she adored flowers, how much she regretted not training as a florist. Between arranging and rearranging the flowers, she'd checked the laying of the tables – straightening a fork here, polishing a glass there, sighting along the rows, making sure everything was in perfect alignment. The ascending tones of her voice reflected the mounting drama of the occasion. Truly this was Henry V on the eve of Agincourt. Saturday would be Sally's day, but Thursday evening quite definitely belonged to the mother of the bride.

Patsy issued words of inspiration and encouragement. Uncle Rex who was in the motor trade reported the hire cars had been ordered, their ETA tallied exactly with the time on Patsy's list. The way she praised his efforts, one could easily have imagined a miracle had been performed.

'There's no way I'll forget the cake,' muttered Geoffrey getting into his car. 'What does Patsy think I am?'

As he drove he thought about Sally. When she was a little girl she'd wait for him to arrive home, her little face looking out the front window, jumping into his arms as he came through the door, whispering in his ear the name she'd given him, 'Mr McMoggy'. She'd sit on his knee as he read to her before dinner or follow him around bubbling with stories about her day. One of her things was to grab hold of his nose and squeeze till his eyes watered – only Sally could get away with that. But over the years, the warmth of that relationship had waned, and now she treated him with almost as much disdain as the rest of them.

That afternoon was like any other second Friday of the

month – a staff training session was being held in one of the smaller courtrooms. As it was the end of the week, the participants were having difficulty hiding a yawn from Old Eagle Eye, as Geoffrey was known. It was clear they could hardly wait for the seminar to end. One of the deputy registrars had been giving a presentation, and Geoffrey was doing the final wrap-up. He would never have used that expression himself, having as he did a hatred of clichés, but after the deputy registrar had purposefully dropped in a few 'bottom lines' and 'level-playing fields' during his presentation, he had finished by saying that Geoffrey would 'do the wrap-up'. He was a bright lad who wore sunglasses in the office. Geoffrey had more than a strong suspicion he smoked marijuana.

Predictably, Geoffrey was now in a foul mood. He stood in front of the group grinding his teeth and waiting for silence. 'Bottom line,' he said at last. 'Bottom of what? *Show* me this bottom line. As for "level playing field", here is another phrase that has no place in any court, where language has to be exact and follow the rules. Clichés lead to sloppy thinking and sloppy work. And haven't you heard the world is round, or perhaps you belong to the Flat Earth Society?' He could allow himself a little sarcasm in situations where he was nominally in control. 'There never has been and never will be a level … Jesus Christ, the *bloody cake!*'

His eyes had risen above the seated heads and were fixed on the large wall clock. *Three minutes past five!* Geoffrey bolted through gaping staff and out through the door. Racing down the stairs, not trusting the lift, he shot out the front door. His watch registered three minutes past. 'It'll be closed! My God, it'll be bloody closed,' he muttered, 'I can't believe it! Don't let it be closed.'

Dashing across the street, weaving his way between lanes of homeward bound traffic, Geoffrey sped along Cuthbert Street and around the corner. The bakery was a mere three hundred metres from the Court, the only reason Geoffrey had been trusted with collecting the cake. Surely …

Closed.

The panicky feeling in his stomach was the same terror he'd experienced as a child when his mother reached up to the cupboard where Mister Strappy lived. Geoffrey leaned up close to the bakery door, mouthing the words there, 'Hours: Mon to Fri, 8.30am to 5pm.' The feeling of nausea and panic was rising to his chest, becoming a physical ache.

He had a thought. One of the shopkeepers around here must know the baker's name and where he lived. He jogged to the hardware store. The usual khaki-overalled gent was there behind the counter. As he explained his predicament Geoffrey observed how little the man had aged in the previous dozen or so years. He sympathised in his North Country accent, said he knew the baker well, that they often chatted, but for the life of him he couldn't recall anything about him – just one name: 'Jim'.

'Try Bruce up at the grocery,' he said. 'He's served

the area nigh on forty year, he's bound to know.'

With renewed hope Geoffrey shuffled the thirty metres to the grocery store. He and the grocer recognised each other immediately; they'd been at primary school together. But there was no time to reminisce. Bruce was most solicitous, could even recall the name of the previous owner. He then remembered the present owner was the son-in-law of the former owner – but of course they wouldn't share the same surname, would they. Bruce reached for the telephone book.

'Bill Chesney, I'll find him in the book, give him a buzz. He's got to know how to get in touch with his son-in-law.'

A spark of hope! But Geoffrey knew not to assume too much, life was full of disappointments, reward came only from determined, painstaking effort. He was aware of the quiver in his voice. 'Perhaps I won't have to go bush after all,' he said. A lame attempt he knew, to make light of such a serious situation.

The grocer eyed him sympathetically, and just as he lifted the receiver he seemed to remember something else. 'You know that vacant shop three doors down from the bakery?'

Geoffrey nodded, he'd noticed it the previous week.

'Jim has set up a temporary business there selling Christmas decorations. They may just be open, this being Friday night.'

'Thank you, Bruce, thank you, thank you! You've been a wonderful help!' Geoffrey rushed from the grocery and headed straight for the Christmas decoration shop. He was no longer running. His legs felt as though they'd turned to mush, requiring an enormous effort to put one foot in front of another. Workers were pouring out of doorways now, blocking his way, oblivious to the urgency of his situation.

The shop door was open. As he staggered into the brightly lit world of glittering tinsel, shiny glass balls, artificial Christmas trees, crackers, plastic snow, all manner of decorations, he was greeted by Jim the baker, strong arms folded across his chest, a broad grin on his ruddy face.

'I've been wondering when you'd turn up, there's this small matter of the wedding cake.'

Geoffrey doubled over, a pain in his chest. Huge relief!

'You look knackered,' said Jim. 'Here, have a seat, I'll get you a glass of water.'

'No thanks, I'll be fine, we'd better just get the cake. Sorry to be such a nuisance.'

Jim withdrew the key from his pocket as Geoffrey followed him at a trot. The pain in his chest was easing. Nice man, thought Geoffrey, feeling quite undeserving of such kindness. Just as they reached the bakery door, they heard a telephone ringing inside.

'Strange,' said Jim. 'Who could be phoning at this hour?'

Patsy had decided at lunchtime that everything that could be done was already done. With time on her hands she began having niggling doubts about the dress she'd bought six months earlier. Off to town she sped for a spot of shopping, an activity she relished. At ten minutes past five driving home around the bays, with several dresses on appro' on the back seat, she had what she believed could only have been a flash of ESP. Patsy's foot pressed down hard on the accelerator pedal. She eventually pulled up outside the garage, negotiated the narrow steps as best she could (she was still carrying too much weight despite her efforts to slim down for the wedding), and trundled along the front path.

There on the veranda sat a familiar figure, head buried in a newspaper. Patsy recognised the shape of her eldest son down from Palmerston North for the wedding. 'Hullo, Brian,' she tossed off as she rushed past. She was in the front door and dialling Geoffrey's work number before her son could rise to his feet.

No reply. Stubbornly she dialled again, still no reply. 'Ah, I'll try the baker,' she said, ignoring Brian's mournful gaze through the open door. She dialled the baker's number and let it ring, and ring, mumbling to herself (and partly to Brian), 'The poor baker must be cleaning his ovens or greasing his pans, or whatever it is bakers do. I must hang on ... Oh, wonderful! You *are* there!'

As the men burst through the door, Jim had reached for the receiver.

'I thought I might have missed you.'

Geoffrey was standing behind Jim. He could hear

every word. The not-so-faint voice had a familiar tone to it.

'It's Mrs Stoddart. Has my husband called for the wedding cake?'

'Yes. For sure, as a matter of fact he's right here. Do you want to speak to him?'

'No, thank you, I just thought he may have forgotten to pick it up.'

'No, no, nothing like that,' said Jim. 'Thanks for ringing, Mrs Stoddart.'

Patsy lowered the hand piece onto its cradle. She wore a puzzled frown. 'It's now twenty-past five,' she said aloud. 'He must have spent at least half an hour with the baker, assuming he got there before five. I hope they haven't been drinking, but that's not like Geoffrey. Goodness knows what he's been up to.'

She returned to the veranda. 'Brian,' she said, bending to give her son a kiss. 'You must be fed up sitting here. When did you arrive?'

And she looked at him full face.

'Aahhh!' she shrieked. 'It's not Brian! *Stuart!* You're supposed to be in London. What a lovely surprise, you've come all the way from London and I've completely ignored you. Sally will be *absolutely thrilled!* Darling, I'm so sorry about just now, rushing past you like that, but you know how useless your father is. I just had this awful feeling as I drove home that he'd forget to pick up the wedding cake.'

And that's when Patsy finally embraced her second son.

*

Geoffrey was on his way home, keeping an eye on the wedding cake. It was sitting on the passenger seat, cartoned up, and securely buckled in. A thought occurred to him as he drove. Perhaps he might be asked to give a speech at the reception? 'Friends and relatives of Sally and Ivan's, I'm honoured to have been entrusted with the procurement of the magnificent wedding cake you see up there on the bridal table. You may or may not be aware that the ceremony which surrounds the cutting and distribution of the cake has ancient, and of course, wonderfully symbolic meanings …'

But he knew he wouldn't be asked to give a speech. And if he suggested it himself he'd be howled down. Even, he feared, by Sally.

Tears rolled down Geoffrey's cheeks, as he continued to drive and watch the cake out of the corner of his eye.

# Weta Man

The Purple Pelican, an anachronism if ever there was one. It's fifty years since Henry Symondson frequented the place with his mates. Back then, he was usually drunk enough to experience the euphoria, forgetting the depression that inevitably followed. Fifty years ago success was the last thing he envisaged.

He hasn't had a drink in years, but his head's reeling as he gazes again at the purple decor, chrome furniture, plastic table covers in mauve and black checks. The music touches a nerve. It's Sinatra, the young Sinatra singing with Tommy Dorsey. Conjures up all sorts of images – wartime, American servicemen, a kid from a poor family scrounging chewing gum.

He examines the meal the waitress slams down in front of him. An enormous steak, tomatoes, mushrooms and chips. No onions, thank God she's got that right. He's wondering where to start when the waitress returns with milky coffee and a plate of white bread, thinly sliced, pre-buttered. The coffee's slopping round in the saucer. Nothing's changed.

'Enjoy,' she breathes, swivelling round, and wiggling her hips as she batters her way through the swing doors.

Symondson pictures vats deep-frying, fat dripping off walls and ceiling. No wonder you needed to be drunk to come to a place like this. He must have been mad hoping this visit could put him in touch with his past, the excruciatingly unhappy, wildly exciting past. Those days had been at the sharp edge of living.

He's about to stand up, pay for the meal and leave without touching a morsel, when the old man sitting at the next table says something. His name's being mentioned. Symondson remains seated.

'Hasn't changed a bit has it, Mr Symondson? Just the same as it was fifty years ago.' The voice has a slight tremor to it.

He noticed the old man earlier – there is something familiar about the face, but then Symondson's lived in this city most of his life so everyone feels familiar. The man is skinny and angular, with close-cropped grey hair and beard; tanned, but a pinched look about him. The most striking feature is the alert, widely spaced, almost black eyes watching from behind steel rims. His clothes – black and beige – are clean but a little shabby, the trousers pressed and the boots polished. Having spoken, Symondson's neighbour continues eating with head tilted slightly, carefully, methodically, cutting small portions and swiftly transferring them to his mouth, giving the impression of a large foraging invertebrate.

Ever since his business activities cast him into the public arena, strangers have occasionally addressed Symondson by name. Nothing unusual about that, but he's wary of getting into conversation, as there's often an agenda, some cause or personal misfortune requiring substantial injections of cash.

'Surely an amazing place,' Symondson growls, head down now, cutting a wide margin of fat from the untouched steak.

'You don't remember me?' says the old man, who has almost finished his meal. 'Our paths crossed fleetingly once, almost fifty years ago. I can't say how much it pleases me to have this opportunity to thank you.'

Symondson's head jerks up. 'Thank me! What for?'

'You were the one who took notice of my predicament, the only one. Do you remember – the suicide, the woman who jumped off the Northern Assurance building?'

The hair on the back of Symondson's neck stands on end.

'As she fell,' says the old man, 'she knocked the briefcase from a pedestrian's hand. I was that pedestrian.'

'I saw the entire thing,' says Symondson putting down his knife and fork, 'but I don't remember you.' This last bit is a lie …

*I'm on the third floor office of the insurance company. The desk is against a wall at a ninety-degree angle from the windows, which face Lambton Quay. Eighteen years old and it's my first job. I'm trapped, trapped and defeated, loathing the work, but what else can I do without years of hard slog and study, and by now all the energy's been sucked out of me. I can't even begin to take the first steps toward making a fresh start, and equally, I'm unable to contemplate the prospect of a future living this way.*

*I resort to alcohol, which gives some relief, but I know it won't stop with a couple of drinks. It's one after the other with my drinking mates till six o'clock when the bar closes. Every evening's the same, shouting slogans and clichés, guffawing loudly at each other, every second word an obscenity. Temporary euphoria, but then the hopelessness of my life sinks in, and disillusionment slips inexorably into black depression.*

*Now I'm looking toward the corner of my bedroom. The hunting rifle standing there is a cut-down service .303. Lying on my bed I can smell the well-oiled barrel. I've tasted that oil, put the muzzle in my mouth, and when I do, I can reach the trigger. I've tried it more than once. I shudder at the thought.*

*I'm sitting at my desk again, late afternoon, a winter's day, and just half an hour till knock-off time. How slowly they move, the hands of that clock. Suddenly within my peripheral vision I'm aware of a large object falling past the window.*

*A muffled thud. I open the window and look down. Shit! A woman's body is lying face down across the pavement, her coat splayed out, one leg bent beneath her, the other sticking sideways at a very odd angle. And beside her, a briefcase.*

*Some idiot's dropped the thing from above, knocking*

*that poor woman over! The pavement's crowded. How could anyone be so stupid at this time in the afternoon? Christ! That's blood running across the pavement and trickling over the kerb! It must have been her that fell, not the briefcase.*

*There's a tableau on the pavement: three or four people stand staring at the body. A man approaches. He's taking a folded newspaper from under his arm, squatting down, laying out sheets of newspaper, covering the woman. He strides off. Seems like a bizarre thing to do, but then I've never before seen a dead person, let alone a suicide.*

The morning after the suicide, the *Dominion* reported that a woman aged twenty-eight fell from a building in Lambton Quay and died in the ambulance on the way to hospital. For days afterwards, Symondson can't get the picture of that young woman out of his mind. What could have made her do it? And what a terrible way to go. How long had she stood on the parapet several storeys above where he sat, waiting to jump? The horror of it made him realise he must take himself in hand, otherwise he too was headed for violent death.

'You don't remember me?' The quavering voice continues. 'You were the only one who spoke to me while I was still in shock. You enquired whether I was all right; took me around the corner for a cup of tea, you even helped me get to my bus. How exceptionally kind you were to me that day.'

Symondson remembers it all perfectly. He'd knocked off at the usual time and walked down the three flights of stairs. The lift attendant lurking on the ground floor motioned toward the figure sitting on the bottom step, and whispered how the briefcase had been knocked from the man's hand when the woman fell, and how he'd been sitting there ever since. The man was pale and hunched over, looking shocked, clutching his briefcase.

Symondson had felt sympathy then, an opportunity had been presented where he could show a softer side to his nature. As a child he'd often stood up to bullies who were harassing younger children in the playground. For some time after the suicide, he'd felt better about himself, and was secretly quite proud of his actions. But some part of him had atrophied long ago. He didn't have time for this.

'I remember that woman, but not you.'

The old man is shaking his head, slowly. 'No. You don't, do you?' It's as if Symondson's part in the event held some particular importance for him. 'I've often seen you around town but I've never had the opportunity to thank you in person. That tragedy happened in 1957, easily the worst year of my life.' Tears are welling up in the old man's eyes and he turns away.

Symondson looks down at his plate. Having heard this much he has a strong urge to put a stop to the old loser's ramblings. For years now he's been careful to shield himself from other people's miseries. His PA takes care of that.

But the old man continues. 'My wife died giving

birth to our only child. They both died.' He pauses. 'That was five months before the woman fell. I was still wretchedly unhappy. She fell that day nearly killing me. It just about finished me off – certainly finished off my career as a scientist. Am I boring you, Symondson?'

Normally Symondson would have shut the old man up with some unkind comment, but he feels a tenuous affinity developing for this person who was present at such an important point in his earlier life. 'Well, I admit it's a surprise meeting you after all these years.'

'Up till then life was going pretty well for me. I had what seemed like a promising career at the university, a lectureship in the zoology department. It was my good fortune to discover a previously unknown species of weta on an island in the Marlborough Sounds. I'd written a paper which was published overseas. The local press got hold of the story and began calling me "The Weta Man".'

Symondson's not at all surprised judging by the old chap's appearance. He's only half listening as the Weta Man goes on with a list of ensuing miseries, how he couldn't hold down a job following the trauma, was hospitalised with depression and anxiety, never married again and so on. Symondson is busy following his own train of thought. The shock of the woman's death was profoundly frightening at the time, and made him realise how precious life was. He stopped the regular drinking, dumped his old friends, began studying, got a job with an accountancy firm, and saved his money.

But Symondson's real break came when he borrowed money, what in those days was a large amount, and used it to buy his first building. He'd sold it within six weeks for twice the original purchase price. After that he became a large-scale property developer. There was plenty of excitement in those first few years, but the satisfaction had worn thin, till finally ... nothing. Shades of the old depression have been haunting him of late. He feels a terrible emptiness.

He notices the Weta Man has finished eating, but is still sitting there as if waiting for some response. Symondson makes a sudden unaccustomed gesture, reaching in his suit jacket pocket for his cheque book. 'Look, can I help you?'

The old man flutters a hand, 'No, no, that's very kind. No, I don't need financial help, or any sort of help, really. And you already helped me enough all those years ago, probably much more than you'll ever realise. You were one of the first people to introduce me to compassion. You, and several of the regulars who came here to the Purple Pelican. Many of them are dead now – we're talking about a long time ago, aren't we? No, I'm actually quite comfortably off in my own modest way. If you've got a minute, I'll tell you the rest of my story.'

Symondson, who has cringed inwardly at the word 'compassion', is recovering from his blunder at not reading the situation correctly. He berates himself for breaking a long-established rule never to offer handouts without a thorough investigation, another thing the PA takes care of. He makes a point of looking at his watch, but he's already decided to listen. There's a quality about the old man he finds interesting. A confidence, and an inner strength and serenity, beneath this embarrassingly open need to unburden himself.

'I suppose I could spare a couple of minutes.'

'I've told you how I couldn't go back to being a scientist. It was in this place, here in the Purple Pelican, that I found my second career. One of the regulars was a painting contractor, he was short of men and asked me if I'd give him a hand finishing a job. That was my introduction to painting and decorating. I found I had a skill for it – you need to be careful and accurate – and my training as a scientist helped, but I also had a flair for colour schemes. I loved transforming houses and seeing the delight on the faces of their owners. It put me in touch with the desperately unhappy lives of some of them. Yes, even some of the rich.

'They found me a good listener if they decided to talk about their lives. That's where I discovered the power of compassion. The interesting thing was realising that I seemed to be getting as much out of it as the people who were unburdening themselves. So my second career brought me rewards far beyond my expectations. I loved the work, got a reputation as a genuine craftsman, was quite sought after in fact. And – this part you'll no doubt appreciate – I was able to charge a premium for my skill and my flair for colour.'

He's very good at promoting himself, Symondson thinks.

'You might say, like many insect species, I've adapted perfectly to my environment. And the regulars here in the Pelican, they became my family – and the few that are alive today still are. You may regard them as a motley crew, but there have also been some quite well-known people who've come to love the atmosphere in this place. There must be something … the food's not up to much is it?' The Weta Man smiles at Symondson, lowers his head, and scrapes together the remaining morsels on his plate.

As Symondson leaves the Purple Pelican he's surprised by an unaccustomed feeling of contentment. He recalls again that first encounter with the Weta Man all those years ago. The lift attendant gesturing toward the man sitting shocked on the bottom step having narrowly escaped death. Symondson putting his arm round the man to gently lift him to his feet, doing up his coat buttons, then avoiding the pool of blood on the pavement as they walked round the corner for a very sweet cup of tea.

Henry Symondson's been looking for something to fill the void in his life, and in some strange way he's been led to revisit the Purple Pelican. The Weta Man has shown him something that he has yet to fully comprehend. Compassion, that's not for him. But Symondson remembers again the feeling of self-worth that rose up in him following the small favour he did all those years ago.

# Life As a Minestrone

Believe it, I've seen a vision, no – not a ghost. I'll swear it was real! Three weeks after Jean died, I was here in this chair on the point of nodding off, when there she was coming down the stairs just like she used to, with a cheeky little smile on her face. I tried getting her attention but she ignored me, just turned away and continued on toward the kitchen. She was wearing a hat. That's strange, Jean never wore hats. Her hair was her most attractive feature.

After that I had a visit from the minister lady who'd officiated at the funeral. She went to great pains to reassure me I wasn't going nuts, which of course I already knew. She said it's not uncommon for people who've just lost someone to have this sort of thing happen, what she called a hypnagogic experience. Strange word that, can't find it in my dictionary.

I couldn't tell the children. They've been trying

to shunt me into one of those old peoples' homes. Imagine me, the old rooster crammed in with a bunch of desiccated battery hens. I'll be buggered if they'll get me into one of those places. They thought I must be lonely – lonely now as well as loony. Not likely, I've got my thoughts and memories, even been thinking about writing a memoir; and I've got a whole wall full of books within easy reach. Sometimes I'll sit here all day nodding off, waking, nodding off again, not really aware of time – what does it matter?

Who cares, so long as I'm warm enough and my stomach's not crying out for a feed, or I need to go for another pee. This arthritis can make all that getting up and down a bit of an ordeal anyway. Nothing to do with the whiskey of course. Must be all the tea I've been drinking.

I'd be really content, but for the thing Jean said just before she died. It's interfering with my determination to make a start on those memoirs. Could it be she had an affair? I can't think what else it could mean. Jean an adulterer! And if so who with? I found a Saint Valentine's Day card years ago. Yes, and the handwriting looked very, very, familiar. Now that's one big fat clue.

It was just after Jean's little encore that I started mulling over some other ghostly experiences I'd had as a small boy. The first was when Blue Mouse appeared. I would have been four years old, it's one of my earliest memories, certainly one of the clearest considering it was so long ago.

I was in my parents' bed, very early morning. Their

bed was enormous, always so warm and comfortable, and that morning I had it all to myself, the bedside lamp casting a soft glow. When suddenly there was this blue mouse travelling steadily across the room, just above the level of the pictures. He was a sort of translucent blue, and although he looked like a mouse, he was about the size of your small domestic rat. (Not liking rats I've always thought of him as a mouse.)

I didn't know what to make of this Blue Mouse business. I wasn't afraid, thought he was rather wonderful in fact. I'm wondering if I should put this sort of thing in the memoirs. Better not, they already think I'm a few bricks short of a load. Anyway, no one at the time explained what was happening and why I was in my parents' bed at such an early hour with the light on. Little children take stuff like that for granted. It turned out I was about to embark on the biggest adventure of my young life.

My dad had borrowed a car – not many people owned them in those days – and we were going on the long drive from Wellington to Auckland. It was quite a trek, and my parents must have wanted to set out early so I could sleep part of the way. They were getting ready for our departure, and I'd been deposited in their bed so as not to disturb my brothers. It was my turn to visit the grandparents, the first time we'd met in fact.

I've got memories of that trip north – the clear, golden, early-morning light on dew-laden paddocks and patches of bush. Steam rising off the land. Sheep, cows, horses, pigs were all new to me, a city kid – so you can imagine the wonder of it all. In those days there was still evidence of the great fires and bush clearances of the previous century, particularly in the middle of the island. Charred and rotting tree trunks and stumps in the paddocks. How's this for memory? We stopped somewhere for breakfast and had sausages with toast and marmalade.

Every few years I conjure up that vision of the Blue Mouse. It always makes me smile when I think about the little chap. My other childhood experience like this was decidedly spooky. The Lady with the Tortoiseshell Cat. Unlike the mouse, she was very frightening; so terrifying I thought she must be a witch. Yes, the Lady with the Tortoiseshell Cat just stood staring at me in this menacing way. She had the palest of pale skin, and light ginger hair just like her cat. I was afraid she was going to run off with me. I'd been listening to stories about gypsies stealing children. Creepy old tart, she reminded me of my first teacher, another witch with ginger hair.

I'll have to turn off the heater. Ah, that's better. Hell's bloody bells, this place is a shambles, Jean would be horrified.

Where was I? Ah yes, I'd been working on this hypnagogic caper ever since I'd seen Jean; thought it might be interesting to experiment with, see if I could make her reappear. I've been wanting her to come clean about this affair business. In my former life I was known as a bit of an expert in the dark arts of cross-examination. And I do miss having her around, even though we spent most of our lives rowing over bugger all. I tried concentrating my mind as I was dozing off, in that twilight zone between sleeping and waking. Didn't work – funny that. Perhaps Jean's had enough of me. Fifty-nine years is a long time.

It's strange the way things turn out. Instead of Jean, who should pop-up but little Blue Mouse! I hadn't seen him for nearly eighty years, but he was much as I remembered him. The little rascal's a bit flighty but very friendly, so I've been encouraging him to visit as often as he likes. I suppose you're thinking I'm like a little child with my imaginary friend. Not the same thing at all. More likely in my semi-comatose whiskey-addled state, I'm talking back to myself, talking to my alter ego. Whatever, I don't really care.

I actually *see* Blue and we have these interesting conversations about all sorts of things: philosophical discussions, finer points of the law, anything and everything under the sun. If you're wondering whether other people have these experiences, of course they do, but they're probably too embarrassed to talk about them, frightened that people will think they've slipped a cog in the brain department.

I met this old chap once, a French professor, wonderful old gentleman he was. Here I go again. We hadn't been in conversation more than a few minutes when he must have guessed I was as nutty as he was, so he tells me about his encounter with the Virgin Mary. It probably wasn't a hypnagogic experience in the true sense of the word, more like a vision. It happened a long time ago when he was eight years old. His mother'd sent him out to get a bucket of coal, and that's when the Virgin Mary appeared in the darkened coal shed. Beautiful, all white and radiant.

When he told his mother what he'd seen she boxed his ears. You see she was an atheist and an anarchist, and her son seeing the Virgin Mary was the last thing she wanted to hear. I like that story. What I particularly liked was the way he laughed as he told it, laughed till the tears rolled down his cheeks. People take these things far too seriously.

That's a fair bit to go over at one sitting. I can feel a little zizz coming on. This could be one of those times when I see the little fellah. Well, stone the sparrows and green cockatoos! If it's not Little Blue from Timbuc–

'What have you been up to, George?' He says. He's hovering just above the TV today.

'That's none of your business,' I say. 'Now don't look so hurt. Jean used to say what a rude old bugger I was. Sorry, Blue. I was just doing a bit of rehearsing. Between you and me, I've begun writing my memoirs. Nothing so grand, really, just a few notes for the children and grandchildren to ponder when I'm gone. A bit of … bit of … can't think of the word.'

'*Conceit* – is that the word you're looking for?'

'Yes, that's it: conceit. What would I do without you, Blue? Anyway sit down and take the … no, no, weight isn't a problem for you, is it?'

'Are you starting with your childhood, George?'

'Probably, that's what I've been playing around

with. D'you reckon that's the sort of thing that would interest them?'

'To be sure. What about the distinguished life of George Adams QC, your journey through life.'

'Cut out the sycophantic nonsense, and that "journey through life" stuff, the metaphor's been done to death and it's straight-line thinking. Life's not like that, Blue. Life's a minestrone.'

'A minestrone! That's a funny way to think about life, as a minestrone.'

'Ah no, not when you consider the things that go into a minestrone. First the ingredients you have control over in the regular recipe, and then there's all the extra bits you throw in at the last minute. Everything combines to produce a unique flavour, you never know how it's going to turn out. Sometimes you get a nasty surprise, like when someone tells you some garbage just before they die, and you can't work out what they mean. Then there's the random way the bits float round in the liquid; it's never quite the same arrangement twice. But sometimes, if you use your imagination and look closely, there's a pattern, a symmetry. And there are attractive-looking minestrones, but mostly they look a complete and utter mess.

'Minestrones don't last long either – they get chewed up and swallowed, and sometimes spewed out. Like our place in this great wide universe, it's all over in the twinkling of an eye. Life's a minestrone, Blue, believe me, I know about life. And I'm something of an expert on minestrones, in case you hadn't noticed. I'm forever brewing one up these days. They don't need much mastication, the old chompers being in dire need of refurbishment.'

'You're pretty cynical about life, George, getting chewed up and spewed out.'

'Not at all, Blue. In fact I've felt perfectly contented in recent years, very much at peace with myself, floating along in the great scheme of things, prepared to face up to the inevitable. You might say it's a type of faith, but not your conventional religious sort. You won't catch me believing in a life after death or any of that nonsense. When it ends, that's it, mate. Curtain down, no encores. Though come to think of it, Jean's had a sort of encore hasn't she? Which reminds me, Blue – something's been on my mind these last few weeks. Perhaps you can help. It's to do with Jean. I've been fretting about something very strange she said before she died. Quite out of character it was.'

'What was it, George?'

'Two days before Jean died, I was sitting with her – now don't you go chirping this all around Mouse Town – and she was quite wide awake and rational, when suddenly she said, "George, dear, do you think I'll be punished for deceiving you?" And then she turned over and faced the wall. I can tell you, it took the steam right out of the old engine, so much so I didn't give her a chance to explain properly what was on her mind. I simply said, "There's no question of punishment, I'm quite sure about that, and even if there was it wouldn't happen to a good person like you." Looking back afterwards I realised she must have been pretty troubled about something, and now I'm having terrible regrets I didn't find out what it was that was weighing her down.'

'She was religious, then?'

'No, at least I never thought she was. I always thought of her as an atheist, or at very least agnostic. That's what makes this talk about punishment all the more peculiar. And there were a few words she spoke as she was dying two days later. She said, "George, don't worry, I should have told you," then she mumbled a couple of phrases. My hearing's not too hot and she was very weak by then. I'm afraid I didn't catch what she said, but it must have been some sort of confession. What do you think she meant? *Blue!* Where have you gone?'

The little bugger disappeared, just when I needed him! What's that? Good God! It's Jean coming down the stairs again wearing that little enigmatic smile.

'Jean, Jean, answer me, Jean. You had an affair didn't you? That's what you meant when you said you'd deceived me. I remember finding that Saint Valentine's Day card from Dickson. Must have been thirty years ago. Did you have an affair with that little twerp?'

'No, George dear. Nothing like that, I was never interested in Dickson – don't insult me. But I did deceive you. It went on for years. Remember how I always said how mean you were over the housekeeping money? Well, you were. I had to wheedle it out of you, and you calling me a spendthrift. But in a way you were right, George. I had an addiction. He! He! Every time I went to town I indulged my addiction. Climb up to the attic, if you can make it on those crook knees of yours, and have a look. You'll find clues up there.'

Took me a while to digest that lot. I had to pour myself a Scotch, and then another – and another, the idea being to anaesthetise the old knees prior to the assault on Everest. She'd really cranked up my curiosity.

Yes I made it, hadn't been up there with the cobwebs for decades. You'll never guess what I found? No, not a bunch of love letters from a secret lover. No, not a Dorian Gray-type picture. Not even the equipment of a dominatrix. Wait for it … I found dozens of brown paper bags filled with hats. Hats! For God's sake! That's what she'd been hoarding all these years, would you believe it? A small fortune tied up in hats. Do you think she'd go up there and put those frilly, fanciful, frightful things on, all manner of shapes and fashions, and parade around in the attic? Probably!

'Well, I'll be. You're a strange one! Life's a minestrone all right, Jean. And I was a mean bastard.'

She's fading.

'Jean, come back! I miss you terribly.'

'I miss you too, George.'

# Happy New Year

Some way to spend the holidays, thought Andrew as he watched the flash of goldfish in the murky water. He'd been trying to catch these fish ever since they'd arrived at the guest house.

'Andrew! Andrew! Where are you?'

Blast, it's Mum, she'll spot what I'm up to. Andrew attempted to hide, moving behind a clump of rushes.

'Andrew, what are you doing down there? Not getting into mischief I hope.'

'Just lookin' for frogs. I'm going down the beach.'

'Look-ing, not lookin'. You really must learn to speak properly. And, it's not a good idea to go to the beach this morning – it really is a bit too cold and windy. Why don't you go and play with the other children? There's a girl about your age. What's her name – ?'

Andrew looked around to see if anyone else was watching. Cupping his hands he carefully slid them into the water. The pond was the smallest of three in a part of the garden completely shaded by large old pōhutukawas. Ugly, rough, concrete paths and low walls lead down to the ponds. Andrew thought even the plants were ugly – they were all the same colour with purple flowers, and the leaves had masses of holes eaten out of them by the woolly black caterpillars. He could see lots of them crawling all over the leaves and stalks.

Those other kids are just a bunch of babies, he thought. Except for Penny that is. Crouched beside the pond Andrew could see through the trees to a sunny lawn. Several guests were gathered on deck chairs, chatting. Penny was there too. He'd fallen in love with Penny, he knew it must be that, but the trouble was he couldn't think how to begin a conversation with her. *Say, doll, you're the best looking gal around these parts.* Or … *where've you been all my life, sweetheart?* Nah, the things the American film stars said somehow wouldn't be right.

Every time she was anywhere near he felt funny, he knew he was blushing and he hated that. Although her name appeared almost constantly in Andrew's thoughts he'd never once said it aloud.

Some distance from the group on deckchairs, sat the woman with the pale-faced little boy who never left her side. She was the saddest person Andrew had ever seen. His dad said they were Jewish refugees who'd escaped from the Nazis just before the war.

Beside her, Penny shone – she didn't look at all sad.

She had short dark curly hair and tossed her head as she moved about chatting with the grown-ups. She was enjoying herself, and the adults were smiling and laughing at the things she said. His mother said Penny read all sorts of books, sometimes even adult books, and said he should ask Penny about the book she was reading now, the one called *Withering Heights*.

Just then it started pelting down, a sun shower, the big raindrops making hundreds of little ripples on the pond. Andrew watched as the guests on the sunny lawn scurried for cover, the women squealing and pulling their cardigans down, or wrapping arms around the blouses of their summer dresses. The men were guffawing and shuffling about, guiding the ladies under sun umbrellas. Crikey, thought Andrew, those men, if they only knew how silly they looked.

The sun shower only lasted a couple of minutes. His jersey smelt of wet wool, but he wasn't concerned about a bit of rain. It was nothing when you thought about what the soldiers had to put up with during the war. Wartime stories of heroism and suffering always made his eyes water. Andrew looked for the sad woman, but she had disappeared. She must have gone inside.

He felt cut off from those other people, the ones sitting in the deck chairs, most of all from Penny. How different they were, the way they talked, quite unlike the words he and his friends shouted at each other across the playground. He didn't have the right words for those people, and anyway they weren't in the slightest bit interested in talking to him. Andrew felt sorry about Penny though. He desperately wanted for her to be his friend.

The next day was New Year's Eve, and there was to be a 'do' for everyone including the children. They'd moved the billiard table down one end of the recreation hall. His mother said there was going to be a dance and, she said (with a hint of drama), they'd hired a pianist and a Master of Ceremonies!

Andrew had never been to a dance and the thought of it left him feeling uneasy. His mother insisted he be there. 'I don't want any arguments either, and you can have a dance too. It's about time you let yourself do a few more things like that. It'll be fun.' His palms went clammy at the thought. He didn't think you could just do that, dance, without having to learn first.

Andrew arrived at the recreation hall with his parents.

'Don't you think it looks wonderful, Andrew,' said his mother, 'with all the lights and Christmas decorations?'

'Oh, yeah, I suppose so. What's that white powder all over the floor?'

'That's to make dancing easier, it helps you to glide your feet along.'

The guests were arriving all dressed up in their best clothes. The women, including his mother, wore evening gowns, jackets or capes, long gloves, jewellery, and carried little purses with shiny beads on them. Some of the men wore dinner suits and bow ties, and what his father said were 'patent leather' shoes.

Andrew watched as Penny came in with her mum

and dad. He couldn't take his eyes off her. Nobody had ever looked so pretty. Her curly hair was all fluffy and shiny, and she was laughing as usual.

As the evening wore on he thought the dance was the worst thing that had ever happened to him. He felt so stupid standing around watching everyone else dancing, and it was even worse when he sat down. It was as if the whole world was looking at him and thinking, 'What a dope you are.' And Penny was dancing with all the men, even his own father, and she hadn't once looked in his direction.

She was lovely in a dress with flowers on it, white socks and shiny leather strap-over shoes, and her tiny pearl earrings caught his eye every time she circled past. She chatted away in her tinkling little voice and seemed to be enjoying herself. Yes, she was having a wonderful time. The grown-ups looked happy enough too, he thought, pleased with themselves, full of their own importance. Some of them were definitely showing off, you could tell by the way they were dancing. Andrew felt miserable.

'You've been sitting here by yourself all evening looking quite unhappy,' said his mother in a loud whisper. 'Why don't you go and ask Penny for a dance?'

He desperately wanted to, but how could he? Penny was a couple of inches taller than him, and if he asked and she agreed what would he do next? And what could he say to her? He felt weak and numb, unable to move without an enormous effort. Andrew lurched down onto a wooden form, gripping its sides.

'If you won't dance with Penny, then perhaps I could help,' said his mother. 'What about you stand up and try dancing with me? I'll show you how and then you can go and ask her.'

It's a good job my friends can't see me, thought Andrew as he was steered around the floor in his mother's firm embrace. This dancing is much harder than it looks. He needed to sit down after that. But endless thoughts continued round and round his mind. Shall I ask her? No I can't. Yes I should. No, I'll only make a fool of myself, she's so different from me. All those people are.

The MC was tall and skinny with a crumpled reddish face and wispy hair. The smart suit and waistcoat he wore looked somehow out of place with such untidy features. Andrew's father had said the MC was a Cockney, and he remembered hearing about the Cockney sense of humour. Certainly this man was trying to live up to that reputation; he was telling jokes between each dance and making everyone laugh. They kept saying what 'a card' he was, that he was 'the life and soul of the party', making the dance 'just hum along'. Andrew supposed the man's jokes were funny, but he didn't feel like laughing, his mind like his body still felt heavy and kind of peculiar.

The next dance was called 'the supper waltz' following which everyone stopped to eat. He picked up a sandwich to give himself something to do, but the thought of asking Penny to dance came into his head again and made his stomach churn. Andrew watched the MC who was standing beside the pianist on the opposite side of the room. He was smoking a cigarette which he held sort of back-to-front, like Russians did in the movies.

Why wasn't he chatting with the guests who thought him so marvellous? thought Andrew. And was Andrew the only one to notice the sneer on the man's face as he glanced round the room? He decided he must be mistaken, the adults obviously thought the MC was a really decent bloke. Just then he stood smiling beside the pianist, and announced there would be three more dances following supper, after which it would be time to welcome in the New Year. The time dragged. At last, the pianist played a volley of chords.

'Gentlemen,' said the MC, 'take your partner for the last waltz!'

A young man, who they said had just returned from the war, strode over to where Penny sat. He gave a small bow and leaned forward asking her to dance. She smiled up at him and sprang to her feet. They whirled, and they whirled, and they whirled around the floor.

How did Andrew feel? Well he was relieved the dance was over and he wouldn't have to risk asking Penny to dance with him, and if she had agreed how that could have gone so badly wrong. He was cross with his mother expecting him to be able to do it, just like that. That was not at all fair of her. He must learn to dance, he decided. He'd get really good at it and he'd show them all what an expert he was.

The pianist broke in with several more chords.

Everyone shouted, 'Happy New Year!' They were all smiling and laughing and everybody started kissing everyone else. 'Happy New Year, Happy New Year! Happy New Year!' Some of the ladies near Andrew came up and kissed him, and he in turn started looking for people to kiss. This is not so bad, he thought. Quite fun really. I'm no longer feeling awkward and stupid. He was beginning to forget himself, in fact, and thinking it wasn't so hard after all. Dare he look for Penny? *Kiss her perhaps.* Dare he?

Just then Andrew found himself facing the MC. Without a thought, he stretched up and kissed the man on his chin. 'Happy New Year!' he said in his brightest voice.

The MC stiffened, took a step backward and glared. 'Don't you kiss *me*, sonny! Boys don't kiss men. If you want to *kiss* someone, you go *kiss* your mother!'

A dreadful feeling of shame flooded Andrew's entire being. He was sure everyone in the room must have seen what he'd just done, and they must all now, including Penny, be staring at him in horror. But he didn't look to find out. With eyes downcast Andrew slunk out into the cold night air.

How could he ever face those people now? He would never kiss anyone – ever again!

# Comeuppance

Big problem. How to get even with that disaster of a neighbour. Cathy says I'm obsessed and perhaps she's right. Lionel's been at me for weeks trying to offload a couple of stroppy heifers, and he's almost succeeded in wearing me down.

'They'll keep your grass in order, old chap,' he's been saying, in the clipped tones of what sounds like an English country – ahem – gentleman. 'I've been looking at your paddocks lately and thinking those heifers are *just* what old Frank needs to keep his grass down. Perfect little mowers they'd be. Could do you a first rate price for the little beauties.' This, for the umpteenth time.

I'd better hold on to a vision I have of those heifers bashing their way into our vege garden, and trampling around in the orchard. Wanting us to take them over would have nothing to do with them breaking down

Lionel's fences would it? He'd have bought those cows for a song, knowing him.

Such a shame to let him get to me on such a perfect spring day. I'm lying on my back, propped up by the elbows, at the place where the ground rises gently just below our little pine plantation. I've spent the morning wandering through the trees marvelling at how much they've grown, enjoying the patches of shade and sunshine. Lionel's right about one thing, this grass is getting away. I lie back in it, and look up to see the rusty-coloured seed heads, those feathery heads which hold the dew so wonderfully. Very early morning is always best, the pinky sky reflected in a myriad of tiny pearls. It must be mid-morning now, there's a pleasant warmth in the sun.

*Screech! Thunk!*

Oh God, I know that sound only too well. He's clambering over our boundary fence again, ignoring the stile I built recently in the vain hope he'd use it. Come to think of it, installing a stile was his suggestion. I drop down deeper into the long grass. If I keep very still he might just miss seeing me. The wild turkey nesting few metres away starts her chortling. I carefully raise my head a fraction. He's still not looking this way, must have important things on his mind.

Ever since Eleanor took off, Lionel can't keep away. He must have fond memories of when the two of them lived in our house as newly-weds. Just about every time he comes over he'll do a circuit of the place peering in at all the windows, and if the sun's reflection interferes with his view he'll think nothing of pressing his nose hard up against the glass.

We had fair warning what this man is like when he sold us the property. We'd been looking for some land, no more than a couple of acres, large enough for a decent garden, an orchard, and perhaps a small grove of trees. Cathy had this idea of running a few chooks, there'd be plenty of room for chooks on two acres. But ten! Not on your life – till Lionel persuaded us into buying exactly that.

'You don't want a place like this,' he said. 'Not your style at all, a place like this.'

Bloody nerve! I said to myself. I'll show you what I like or don't like, you fat toad. As it turned out the same thing was going on in Cathy's head. We signed up there and then to ten acres, and Lionel as a neighbour. Still, we love the house – one of those old farm houses with verandas round three sides and wisteria trailing along the roof line. It couldn't be prettier. And it came with various useful outhouses and sheds. Lionel had recently subdivided and built himself a pretentious house on the other ten acres. The house is clad in every imaginable material: natural wood, marble, stone, brick; it has lots of different angles, and of course a couple of classical pillars supporting the portico at his front door. Far too big for a man on his own.

I'm hearing sounds on our veranda, the screen door flying back, muffled voices. Lionel and my wife. Whoa, he's a brave man. Cathy will be furious, she's busy doing some bottling this morning. When Cathy gets steamed up all hell can break loose! He'll have come over thinking he's going to worry me into buying those cows again.

Lionel's always tricking me into doing things I wouldn't normally do. Like the time last summer when it was so damned hot, he got me dipping his lambs …

'I say, Frenk old chep,' he said in that constipated voice. 'A couple of my lembs have got fly-blow. Would you like to come and see what to do, old men?'

Why couldn't he speak in a good honest Pommie accent, or wherever it was he came from? Bah!

I'm no farmer but learning what to do could come in handy, I thought. Lionel's no farmer either, but he's been at it a while longer than us.

'Sure, I'll change my clothes, be right over,' I said.

'And, Frenk, bring that galvanised iron baby's bath from the old wash-house.'

Giving me orders! Ah well, I thought, this could be what's called getting experience.

I arrived over at his place. All the sheep were in one small paddock. You didn't have to be an expert to see what a mess they were in. The scruffiest bunch I'd ever seen; several hadn't lost their tails, some old ewes had missed the last shearing, and all were disgustingly daggy. Of course, like everything else, he'd have bought them for sweet Fanny Adams.

'Okay, you've got the bath, then. Good,' he said. Learning from the ground up can involve a bit of fetching and carrying, I guess. So, I'm excusing my gullibility. 'Now, Frenk, what does it say on the can? I've left me jolly glasses down at the house.'

'Two-fifty mills per five litres of water,' I read out.

'Right, if you'd fill up the bath from that trough over there. 'Fraid I can't lift anything at the moment, doctor's orders, got a hernia or two.' I'm several years older than Lionel and I was struggling with that bath full of water. 'How much gunk do we put in again, old man?'

'Two-fifty mills per five litres,' I repeated, while pouring half a can into the bath, a rough estimate. I suddenly felt the need to get this operation out of the way as fast as possible. Being Lionel's dogsbody was not my idea of having a good time.

'Now, if you'll just catch that lamb over there, yes, the one with the tail still attached. Ah, thanks, old chap. A couple of good dunks and we're ready for the next little blighter. What ho!'

My hands were already dirty so thought I might as well continue. What a mug. Three more stinking, maggoty lambs later, I realised I'd completed the entire operation and my dear friend hadn't lifted a finger.

I wasn't going to think about Lionel today, was I? Yeah, well.

Something's disturbing my reverie. It's him, off home again, still hasn't spotted me. Cathy will have given him a flea in the ear. Well, what d'you know, he's using the stile for a change. Stiffling a little giggle I watch him as he places one foot on the first step, then the other to catch up, just like a small child. Straightening up now he's obviously planning the next move. He leads again with his right foot, the other catches up, and so on. I must remember not to go mountain climbing with Lionel. God help us!

It can't have been long after the lamb-dipping episode that Lionel turns up again with another of his clever manipulations. I fall for it every time.

'Frenk,' he said. 'I've been looking at that fence between our properties. Seems to me the wires are getting a bit stretched, and I've noticed a couple of staples missing.'

'You're not telling me a thing.'

'A stile wouldn't go astray down there. What do you think, old man?'

I knew perfectly well what he was up to and, by the sly little smile he gave me, it was as plain as day he did too. I know how hopelessly inept he is – he'd never be capable of constructing a simple stile. There I was rescuing him again. Of course, I was also rescuing our half of the boundary fence. Anyway, I was down there the very next morning cobbling a stile together. Lionel showed up just as I was finishing. He'd have been watching from behind his venetians.

'I say Frenk, you're on the ball, old man. I was just thinking of doing that myself. Done a jolly good job there.' He was crouched over, peering at it like he was some sort of expert. I was sorely tempted to plant my boot fair up his fat arse.

There are always problems with boundaries – both

physical and psychological boundaries – where Lionel is concerned. A classic example happened at the end of last year. It was Christmas Eve and I was doing my usual surveillance of these little pines, when I came across one that had been lopped off at ground level. There was a telltale trail of flattened grass leading to the nearest point on our boundary fence.

When I'm anywhere near our boundary that pair of cows comes racing over. Black Angus – black devils rather – they follow my every move, rushing back and forth. Buy them, the hell I will!

Anyway, that night we were invited over for drinks. Lionel greeted us at the door and said in his most confidential tone. 'Would you like to view something really special?' We were handed a mulled wine and led into the lounge to join the other guests … There standing in one corner, was the most expensively decorated tree you've ever seen.

Have you ever tried to accuse someone of thievery when they're standing up real close, looking you straight in the eye in the middle of a room full of strangers? His eyes were popping with excitement, and there was that knowing little smile twitching round his rubbery lips. I took a swig and damned nearly choked on my wine.

Old Lionel never fails to surprise, but the most astonishing thing about him was his erstwhile wife. Eleanor was an unsophisticated country girl – pretty, yes definitely pretty, she'd have been twenty, if not twenty-five years his junior. My bet is he'd tricked her into saying 'yes' with the same sales technique he used on us when we bought the place. Reverse psychology, I believe it's called. When Eleanor got to know us a little she began dropping hints that all was not well. She'd catch Cathy on her own and pour out a string of complaints about Lionel's obvious, and not so obvious, shortcomings.

Anyway, she took off one day with this younger guy, the local handyman – the sort who did all the usual agricultural things, a bit of fencing, shearing in season. Lionel could have done with his help in fact. We both felt sorry for Lionel, he completely went to pieces. For weeks he'd sit slumped on our couch pouring out his misery. He couldn't understand Eleanor, he'd given her everything hadn't he? Like that new kitchen fitted out with the very latest appliances imported from Germany, the very best stuff available.

These visits prompted me to get outside and do some long overdue chores. I'd leave poor Cathy to deal with Lionel. To be honest, I can't stand other people's misery. Cathy, bless her, has a heart of gold, despite her sometimes fierce demeanour. Her patience with Lionel over his long period of mourning was quite astonishing.

Last month – let's see, it would have been eighteen months since Eleanor left – we got this idea about one of the sheds. It had probably been a large army hut and would, we reckoned, convert nicely into a bunkroom for the grandchildren when they visited. It wouldn't take much to Gib-out, and the power was already connected. A couple of panes of glass were missing from a window, and pushed up against it was a heavy old wardrobe. We'd skirted round it many times but never bothered taking a closer look. It was one of the pieces of junk Lionel and Eleanor had left behind. The matchwood back was riddled with borer, probably only good for the bonfire.

First thing we did on the day set aside for the clean-up was to haul out the old wardrobe. The doors had been left slightly ajar, and several generations of starlings had nested in this particularly grand nesting box. Cathy sensibly was dressed in old clothes, her hair tucked into a scarf, a necessary precaution against the dust and debris floating around. Despite the old clothes, Cathy still managed to look gracious. Her slim figure helps. Having scraped out this accumulation of droppings and straw, we turned our attention to the bottom drawer. Sliding it open, there to our amazement, wrapped in tissue, neatly folded and hidden from view for, well, I don't know how long, was a pristine white wedding dress!

There's no doubt to whom it had belonged. You couldn't help but wonder at what stage in their marriage poor little Eleanor had decided to hide it away. And later to abandon it in the old wardrobe. Cathy, who had been quite moved by this discovery, thought there was a lot of symbolism in the act of abandoning it like that. We both quite enjoyed the drama, but we were in something of a quandary. Still are.

We have no way of contacting Eleanor, and Cathy

refuses to let me give the dress to Lionel fearing it would plunge him into another fit of depression, and another round of sitting on our couch pouring out his anguish. That dress has been on my mind since the day we found it. I've been indulging in some little fantasies. Cathy keeps asking what I'm smiling about. It's wonderful, at last I've got some power over Lionel.

Fantasy number one: Lionel gets togged up in the thing. He's wearing a wig, bright orange lipstick plastered across his crooked little mouth, and is teetering around on high heels behind his venetians. Then there's the one where he's all cuddled up in bed, sucking his thumb while hugging the dress. In another, I present it to him, he looks startled and then lets out a howl of anguish like a donkey braying. Clutching the dress to his chest, he rushes off across the paddocks braying at the top of his lungs.

I wasn't going to think about Lionel today, was I?

I'm still here soaking up the sunshine, feeling a little guilty, with Cathy inside down there doing her bottling. I think I might just drop off for a little zizz. I can smell the grass and the pine trees, hear the turkey mother rustling around her nest, see above me the little puffy white clouds in the bluest of blue skies. I close my eyes ... drifting off ...

*Screech! Thunk!*

There he is now.

He's heading for our place again, interfering with my little rest. What a hide that man's got. It can't be more than half an hour since Cathy sent him packing.

If I'm not fed up with that stupid bugger. Right, I've had enough! Now's my opportunity. Lionel's about to get his comeuppance.

Watch out, neighbour. Here I come.

I reach the veranda door just ahead of him. I'm excited, yes, quivering in anticipation. I feel like I'm an international football star thrusting my fist into the air having just scored the winning goal. The fans go wild!

'Just a second, Lionel,' I say. 'I've got something for you, something we found.' I rush inside and retrieve the dress from our linen cupboard. I'm back at the door in a trice. There's been no time to consult with Cathy – anyway, she's still engrossed in her bottling.

I hand the dress to him. He looks at it, buries his nose in the fabric, holds it up, turns it around toward the light. 'Lovely embroidery around the neckline. That dress cost me a lot of money,' he says. Not the slightest show of emotion. And you'll never guess what dear old Lionel said next.

'Look old chep, why don't you keep it and give it to that youngest daughter of yours. I suppose she'll be wanting to get married one of these days. Now about these jolly cows, Frenk …'

# Insurance (A Bar Story)

Isometimes tell this story in bars. Depending on how long I can eke it out, it usually earns me a beer or two – sometimes even three. The protagonist is currently doing a long stretch as a guest of Her Majesty. I may as well make the most of it while I can, because when he gets out I'm going to have to disappear – all down to the ineptitude of a certain lawyer I entrusted with some vital bits of evidence. I'm supposed to be under the Police Protection Scheme, but I haven't much confidence in that.

'Fill your glasses, gentlemen, and settle back for the ride. Here goes then:

'Sir David Bartholomew – of course you've heard of him: Australian multimillionaire industrialist and philanthropist? You used to occasionally see him on TV, particularly when he visited this side of the Tasman. Then he became even more famous during the recent trial. Prior to that, didn't people think it was a little strange an Aussie pouring so much money into New Zealand charities and sports organisations?

'*I* knew why, way back. In fact, other than Sir David himself, I was probably the only person living at that time who did – until some of it came out at the trial. I knew his true identity. I recognised him several years before when his face started appearing on our television screens – despite the plastic surgery, his hair line, the nose job, and somehow I wasn't all that surprised. You see, Sir Dave and I went back a long way. "Sir David", I've always had difficulty with that. Even now I still think of him as Syd Chapman. And don't be fooled by his bland appearance. This man can be utterly ruthless.

'Sydney Chapman and I were at school together. A funny-looking little kid, his face somewhere between cherub and gargoyle, chin and nose gravitating toward each other, chubby rosy cheeks, and lips like sweetheart bows. The twinkle in his eye reflected a mischievous nature. Syd was always into some sort of trouble, yet invariably he charmed his way out of it.

'I first noticed his flair for business as an eight-year-old. Syd stole his grandfather's ancient single-barrelled Browning shotgun and hid it under a pile of branches at the back of the Chapman's large property. He advertised his acquisition as an 'elephant gun' – God knows where he dredged that up. Anyway, you can imagine what a bunch of little boys thought about those magic words. Syd collected sixpence to hold, cock, and fire the 'elephant gun' – without cartridges of course.

'When his parents gave him roller skates, the envy of the other kids, Syd claimed to have had them stolen. Straightaways the doting parents replaced the skates. Armed now with two pairs, he hired them out by the hour. He was always into some moneymaking scheme. Paper rounds and milk runs were for plodders, Syd used his brains and charm. I guess I was envious of his ability to make money, even then.

'Later on Syd was given a couple of pairs of boxing gloves, and I became his sparring partner, though "punch bag" would be a more accurate description. He had outstripped me in height, and was almost a head taller. Against a reach like that I didn't stand a chance.'

Okay, here I pause and point –

'Take a look at my flattened nose. You may wonder why I let him use me like this. Well, I must have calculated the advantages outweighed the injuries I sustained. Syd had money for sweets, ice-creams and Coke, provided I'd gone three or four rounds. Later it was for rides in his old man's car which Syd always had liberal access to. But there was more to it than that – excitement always surrounded Syd, excitement and danger. Looking back, that was the main attraction. Anger toward him didn't really surface till later. I'd also forgotten until we met again more recently, how generous and charming he could be.

'If you've wondered how Sir David got his start – I

mean, making all those millions – you can find out about it in the official biography, that is if you enjoy a good read of fiction. I did it differently. I delved into my memory, did a bit of my own research, and put two and two together. And then I developed a plan of my own.

'It's no secret his first large venture was a franchising operation called "The Big Aussie Pie Machine". What isn't known is how he financed it, and from whence came the idea.

'The real story goes pretty much like this: Syd's dad was a trader who'd started in business during the war, buying and selling whatever he could lay his hands on, some of it black market stuff, or so it was rumoured. By war's end he had import licences and a tidy little foreign exchange quota. Just about everything was in short supply, anyone could sell anything. After the war Syd senior became an import agent which meant he rarely ever saw the goods. I remember Syd boasting that his dad wouldn't know what half the stuff he sold even looked like.

'It was understood that being an only child he would enter the business on leaving school, which he did without having gained any of the usual qualifications. Not that he was unintelligent, it was simply that with the demands of his extra-curricular business deals, and the time spent picking up girls in his dad's large American car, there was little time for the academic life.

'Problems arose when he joined the business, till

then a one-man band. Syd and his dad argued over who would be the front person, the one to make the deals. The dad won that one of course – after all, he'd established the contacts. So, young Syd was relegated to the more mundane part of their small enterprise: doing the paper work and keeping the books. He knuckled down and became good at these operations. I recall a phrase his dad used with his cronies, and even me on occasion: 'That boy Sydney, he's indispensable. *Indispensable!'*

'Syd was having to work harder while the old man played around: women and gambling, he was never one for the booze. Syd was still on a wage and becoming increasingly disgruntled. He used to moan to me about the old man's meanness. It was probably only a matter of time before he did something for himself.

'An opportunity presented itself. The Chapmans went on an overseas trip, and since everyone travelled by sea in those days, they were going to be away six months. I can imagine Syd's dad: 'You'll be in charge, Sydney my boy, and you'll need to become a cheque signatory to pay the bills while I'm away.'

'I've guessed, knowing Syd, what went on in his head. It would have been something like. "Well, Dad, that suits me just fine. I've had a guts-full of this little number, and I reckon by now you owe me big time."

'He and I had remained friends over those inter- vening years. He was still using me, sometimes as a sort of decoy. He'd get hold of a good-looking sheila who'd only go in his car if her ugly mate went along too. It was understood I'd sit in the back seat with the ugly one – keep her distracted – while he was getting on with whatever he could get away with up front.

'I once took the rap for both of us. We'd drunk a lot of beer this particular night, which necessitated having a pee against the side wall of the bakery. That's when we spotted old "Swivel Head" the local cop emerging from the shadows. Confronted by the evidence running across the pavement, I confessed straight off. Not Syd, he fingered me as well and denied any part in the crime. My anger was starting to get the better of me, but Syd seemed quite unaware that anything was wrong.'

This is where I usually pause and complain of having a dry throat. Inevitably, one of my listeners heads for the bar, and returns pronto with a large lubricant, quite appropriately refusing to accept any payment.

'Where was I? Ah, yes ... we were both nineteen around the time his folks went on their trip. I was about to move to Auckland to take up a position as a newly qualified wool classer with the outfit I'd joined. We'd got into a fair bit of mischief over the years, but there was nothing you could call really criminal. The parents, bless them, were barely out of the harbour when Syd was into the bank account. He drew out the entire balance of £37,000 – no small sum in those days.

'He took the *Wanganella* to Australia. D'yer remember the *Wanganella*? It spent seventeen days on Barrett's Reef long before the *Wahine* calamity. Syd tripped around to cover his tracks, changed his name, and deposited the loot in various banks over there. The next move was cutting sugar cane in Northern Queensland. You can read all about that in the official biography; that's where he's supposed to have got his nest egg together, by the sweat of his brow.

'What a laugh! Cutting cane was hard dirty work, lots of Kiwi jokers used to do it in those days. I had a go at it a few months later. Sheer coincidence really – I didn't know Syd had been there briefly before me. Why he chose sugar cane when he'd always avoided manual labour I'll never know. Perhaps it was part of a plan to practice the new identity and cover his tracks.

'It was in the bunkroom one night when Ken, another Kiwi joker, got onto his pet subject. He'd travelled working his passage on ships, and nowhere around the world could he buy the equivalent of a decent Kiwi meat pie. Being an inventive sort he'd worked out a way of making pies in a continuous process. As well, it was to be a wonderful bit of visual marketing with the pie machines set up and operating in shop windows. You see, I heard the same story from Ken when *I* was up there – hence I was later able to make the connection with Syd's wonderful invention, as described in the biography. Poor Ken was slaving his guts out trying to rake together enough capital to build a prototype machine.

'By the time Syd heard Ken talk, he was *Dave Bartholomew* from Tasmania. I can imagine what happened when he heard about the pie project. Dave/

Syd had been there less than a month when he picked poor old Ken's brains, pinched the plans and was off.

'When the parents finally caught up with the fact that their Sydney had disappeared, they flew home in a panic. Syd had left a note: "Don't worry, I'm off to make my fortune in the great wide world, your ever-loving son, Syd – P.S. Something seems to have happened to the bank account." Cheeky sod he was.

'Ouch! It was too embarrassing to contact the police at first, the old man would have looked pretty silly in the eyes of his cronies. His son, the one they'd given everything to, embezzling his own father!

'One of the first things they did was write to me in Auckland. I still had that letter tucked away, kept it in a safety deposit box all these years, had an inkling it could eventually come in handy. The letter was to the point. Mr Chapman said Sydney had disappeared with his entire savings, and did I know his whereabouts? It was the first I'd heard about Syd's disappearance, so I was able to say quite honestly that I was as surprised as they were, and had no idea where he'd gone.

'Quite sensibly, after several weeks when they hoped and prayed the prodigal would return, they went to the cops. He was posted as a missing person – even Interpol was notified. The parents hesitated to lay charges, but finally did so when their anger got the better of them.'

I turn now and speak directly to the assembled group: 'What would *you* do, in the circumstances?' A little audience participation doesn't go astray – helps keep them hooked in, I find.

'Thanks to dear Sydney, the old man was having to get back to some solid graft. Two years later both parents were killed when their car, travelling at excessive speed, hit the end of a bridge on a very straight bit of road. I have my suspicions as to whether Mr Chapman had suicide on his mind, despite the coroner's open verdict.

'Pretty sad, really, though even if Syd had known about his parents' deaths he could hardly have come to the funeral. He was now an orphan, which is what he'd told his biographer anyway. He's quoted as saying his parents died when he was a baby. A grandmother in Tasmania is supposed to have raised him.

'Following his brief spell cutting cane, David Bartholomew took off armed with his, I mean Ken's, idea for the continuous pie machine. Dave was granted world patents from drawings done by a very clever toolmaker. He got components made for the machines, and a small assembly plant started turning out Great Aussie Pie Machines almost as fast as he could write another franchise. I'm not just talking about Australasia – North and South America, UK, Europe, Scandinavia. The colder climates went for what I still insist was a really good Kiwi pie. Central America was a bit of a write-off, probably too hot for mince pies.

'One thing led to another. As franchises mushroomed, the demand for cartons to put the pies into increased. Dave got interested in packaging long before most products were cartoned as they are today. His plant grew, became two, then six enormous factories dotted across South East Asia, where labour costs were remarkably cheap and government regulations almost non-existent. There were bribes to pay of course, but also all sorts of tax dodges shifting profits around. And it didn't stop there. Packaging machinery was next, then his own paper and board mills, followed by forests and real estate, a natural progression. As I understand it, at one time he was rated one of the wealthiest men in the world.

'Little Syd Chapman was on a roll. Do you think he could have had a wee bit of a conscience? The SDB Charitable Trust had certainly spread some big money around over the years, particularly, as I've mentioned, in New Zealand. My bet is he had accumulated so much tax-free dough it was necessary to unload some of it. I reckon it was just a great big money-laundering scam. But perhaps it helped the great man get some sleep at night.'

The old throat's usually getting pretty dry again around this point in the story. I only have to pause and clear it to get the desired response. I ask my listeners: Why did I write all this down? What do you think? (This quite often stimulates a bit of discussion, gives me a chance to get the second beer down the hatch. Refreshed I continue.)

'Now, about my plan that I mentioned earlier, I know some people would use that nasty word "protection" or even "blackmail" – I shudder at the thought. I had in mind rather, a sort of "insurance policy".

'You may remember Sir David came over to present

the Sportsperson of the Year Award a few years back. Fair enough, he's propped up any number of sports organisations in this country over the years. Such public recognition for his largesse was long overdue. I wrote to Sir David when I knew he was coming over. See, I had this plan worked out. I reckoned he owed me for keeping schtum all these years. I was also still quite angry at the way I'd been used and abused in our youth.

'Compared to his lifestyle, my requirements were very modest. I'd always wanted to own a small pub, rather fancied myself as "mine host". A couple of bars and a bit of accommodation somewhere up north would have done. I figured Sir Dave wouldn't have minded giving me the wherewithal to set myself up in a modest establishment. He'd have been welcome to stay free of charge any time he was over. We could have sat in the lounge bar reminiscing about old adventures. I'd have shown him my flattened nose and told him how much I'd enjoyed riding around in the back of his car with all those ugly sheilas.

'And if he'd refused? Well, he didn't know I'd still got his dad's letter written and signed in the old man's unmistakable scrawl. And there was another bit of evidence I had put away in the safe-deposit box. I'm referring to the pewter mug Syd gave me for my nineteenth birthday just before I shifted to Auckland. I didn't touch the thing, never did like drinking out of pewter, and it's got Syd's fingerprints all over it. I came across it amongst my souvenirs, still wrapped up in nice clean tissue paper. It's even suitably engraved: *To Cyril, my old partner in crime, hang in there, mate, Syd.*

'It was eventually produced at the trial. You may ask why the trial was held in this jurisdiction and not in Aussie. The case of course hinged on establishing his real identity. After that was established, the Aussies bowed out, in the meantime anyway. I think they were shrewd enough to recognise the enormous costs involved in collecting evidence and running such a lengthy trial. Talk about the "Wine Box Inquiry". After forensic accountants, lawyers and tax department people had had their little feeding frenzy – and with all the "wiring diagrams", written statements and affidavits etc – the evidence and exhibits could easily have filled several wine boxes!

'To return to my part in this saga. I got quite a surprise when I received this handwritten note back real pronto, inviting me for drinks in his apartment. Of course he kept one here, even though he was over less than two weeks a year. Gives you some idea how filthy rich he was. He seemed pleased to see me: I was quite flattered with him turning on the charm and hospitality like that. We had a good chinwag about old times. I must have forgotten how angry I'd been.

'First off he explained the change of name, said it was because he'd got into a spot of bother in Aussie as a young man – nothing serious he said. He made me promise not to let on. Of course I didn't tell him I knew the real story. By the way, he said not to use the "Sir" so I'd been calling him "Dave".

'Then he offered me the job, said he needed someone he could trust. It suited me since the wife and I
had separated several years before, and the kids were
by then well and truly independent. I became Sir
Dave's driver, though fortunately he didn't insist on
me wearing the uniform like the one before me. And
I did other personal services, like making sure he got
up-to-date financial reports no matter where we were
in the world. And there was his personal luggage to
keep track of. And his favourite drinks to mix – I was
good at that. And, there were the ladies I arranged, all
very discreet of course.'

Time for another, ah … pause. Gets them scuttling
off to the bar again. Don't even need to clear my throat
now. A conditioned response I believe it's called.

'Where was I? I remember. Sir Dave asked me about
his parents' deaths and whether I'd been to the funeral.
I lied, said I went down to Wellington when I heard.
He seemed genuinely touched by that. He'd been
extra nice to me since then, and I got a raise the very
next payday. All of which made it harder to do what I
needed to do.

'The arthritis was catching up and I just didn't have
the energy for that sort of caper any more. So I screwed
up my courage, and told him about the ancient relics
in my possession, and about wanting to retire with a
little nest egg, thanks to his generosity.

'What an idiot I was, knowing how ruthless he
could be. He flew into a rage – real scary! He said
unless his dad's letter and the pewter mug were in his

hands within twenty-four hours I'd be having a little accident. And I knew what that meant.

'God, you wouldn't believe it. The evidence didn't turn up. That stupid bloody solicitor I gave it to several weeks beforehand got his wires crossed. Instead of couriering it to me he'd gone into Plan B mode. Sent it off to the Serious Fraud Office! And the rest as they say is history.

'Any questions?'

# Edward Kingsley

People who knew Edward Kingsley were genuinely surprised that someone as careful as he had succumbed to such an avoidable accident. Some even questioned whether it was a failed suicide attempt, but rejected the idea. If Edward was intent on killing himself, they said, he'd have made a thorough job of it.

He'd become seriously depressed when Cynthia died suddenly. She had been his soulmate for well over half a lifetime. Devoted wife and mother. Lover. They were both virgins when they married, but soon learned to trust each other and allow for each other's needs. Their sex life seldom became boring, which would have surprised a lot of their friends who regarded them both as rather staid.

Edward and Cynthia played tennis and golf, and were quite competitive. They walked regularly, holidayed with the children, often in the National Parks which mostly included a few days tramping. They had similar interests in literature, and above all, they just enjoyed being with each other.

A determined person, Edward was gradually – with some help from friends and family – pulling himself out of the depression that followed Cynthia's death. But there was a limit to how much a private person like Edward would share the depth of his grief. He discovered exercise was the best therapy, and so began his habit of taking long walks both morning and evening, often covering the same ground he'd enjoyed with Cynthia. A tall man he kept himself erect as he walked, the set of his jaw reflecting determination. Some days he pushed himself, striding out swinging his arms, filling his lungs and gradually feeling his body come alive again.

The morning outing usually took him up over the hill, down through the shopping precinct, under the ferry wharf if the tide allowed, then along the seawall – gradually increasing the length of his walk. Evenings he went wherever his mood suggested, often passing the site where his grandmother's house had once stood, now occupied by a service station. He had loved his grandmother, but imagining the old house also reminded him of the family secret, a secret he'd never been fully privy to.

As a child the house had taken on a mysteriously fearful aspect. By fitting together snatches of overheard conversation, he'd deduced that something evil had happened in that house which had involved an uncle and a young neighbour. Whatever it was, the thought of it had contaminated the entire family. After all these years Edward still felt somehow implicated in whatever it was that had occurred there, and the sense of shame attached to the secret, details of which were forever kept from him as a child, but which he still puzzled over, and which dwelt in the back of his mind.

He remembered as a small boy occasionally catching glimpses of a girl, a little younger than himself, who lived in the very grand house next door to his grandmother's modest villa. The large stately house was still there but looked shabby, possibly abandoned, and almost hidden amongst trees and shrubs.

As Edward walked, he realised that he would now have to make a life for himself without Cynthia. An idea came to him that he would have a complete break, get right away for a while. Was he too old to go trekking? Not if he was in good physical shape. Edward collected brochures, had a thorough medical and made a booking for March the following year.

That would have been about now, he realised. What a mess he'd made of everything. The thought of that trek had sustained him as he pictured himself walking misty trails through groves of rhododendrons in bloom, against a backdrop of wonderful mountain scenery. He'd further extended his daily walks, because maximum fitness, he reasoned, could only increase the enjoyment of his forthcoming adventure. As he walked he once again appreciated his surroundings – the lovely gardens in front of the well-maintained, mellow, often quaint old houses. Edward's depression considerably improved.

Then on one of his longer outings he noticed a woman coming toward him. As she approached, she flushed, glared at him and abruptly looked away. At that moment Edward experienced a flicker of recognition. But surely it couldn't be …? It simply couldn't be the same person! She was so changed, and such a terrible transformation. He wasn't absolutely certain, but it seemed she had recognised him as well.

At twenty-three, some two years before he'd met and married Cynthia, Edward had become infatuated by a young woman. They'd been introduced at a dinner dance. She was self-assured and good-looking in a classy way, with long black hair, pale complexion and dark brown eyes. He remembered her delicate hands which had obviously never been involved in any kind of household drudgery. Suzanne.

Edward was smitten but also knew he was out of his depth. He later realised it wasn't Suzanne he'd fallen for, but a picture in his mind of some ideal, an ideal whose qualities he'd foolishly attributed to this young woman. There were so many things about her he admired, she was definitely upper class, had attended an exclusive girls school, had travelled overseas and had even spent six months at a Swiss finishing academy.

Edward was aware the other young people who moved in that circle viewed him as an oddity. He was always too conscious of his manners, more formally dressed than the occasion demanded, unbending in his demeanour, and pedantic in his mode of expression. He'd danced with Suzanne twice the evening they met, which encouraged him to risk phoning the following day. To his astonishment she agreed to go out with him. Edward always acted in a gentlemanly manner on their few outings together. She was a confusing mixture of friendliness and complete detachment, often seeming to focus her attention elsewhere. He was conscious of how stilted their conversations were, but blamed it on his own shortcomings.

The most perplexing thing for Edward was the unbearable tension that at times seemed to hover in the air between them, particularly over any physical contact. Sitting in the cinema he'd debate endlessly with himself on whether or not to attempt to hold her hand. When he finally summoned the courage, she'd firmly pushed his hand away. Parked outside her house on their final date, he'd tried to put his arm around her shoulder, and again he was rebuffed. She'd thanked him for the evening and promptly got out of his car. He phoned several times over ensuing weeks, but some family member would answer and say that she was unavailable. He never saw her again.

For weeks, months, even years later he would find himself thinking about Suzanne, and for years he would have a recurrent dream where she'd fade into the distance as he tried to approach, always the same vision of perfection.

Several years passed, Edward had married Cynthia never having told her about this unrequited infatuation. Then one evening at a dinner party, an old friend was reminiscing when he asked Edward if he'd heard about Suzanne. Edward had no need to say, 'Suzanne who?' The friend was surprised he had not heard the news, and reported she had been diagnosed with schizophrenia. Edward covered up the fact he was shaken by this information.

Many years had elapsed since then, but a major psychiatric illness would explain why she now looked so peculiar, the strange way she was dressed, the slash of vivid lipstick plastered across her mouth, the grey, oily hair which had once been so immaculately groomed.

Almost every day after that, Edward passed the Angry Woman, as he now thought of her. He tried thinking of her as Suzanne but failed to connect the two properly in his mind. He carefully showed no sign of recognition, frightened of a scene, of some outburst from her, but he was absolutely certain she was aware he'd recognised her. These frequent sightings were oppressive, causing Edward to become increasingly agitated and anxious. He varied his route but inevitably she'd come towards him, carrying plastic shopping bags overflowing with all manner of strange items.

Every day his heart would race as he saw her approaching. If there was sufficient distance between them he would cross the road, or turn down a side street. Otherwise he would hold his breath and look straight ahead as they passed, the strain often leaving him feeling nauseous. The charade continued week after week. His walks, which had become such an important part of his life, were ruined. Edward couldn't avoid her, and with increasing frequency her wretched face would creep into his thoughts.

He began to wonder whether anything involving him all those years before could have contributed to her breakdown, some attitude, something he'd said or done which could have tipped her over the edge. At a rational level he knew this was ridiculous. Nonetheless he felt guilty; her attitude and angry looks fed the growing belief that she must blame him in some odd way for her condition.

Edward became completely obsessed, waking at 3am to puzzle over his predicament. How could he avoid her? Was she perhaps following him? But that was impossible, they almost always met coming from opposite directions. How could he rid himself of this unfortunate creature? Perhaps one day she'd simply disappear – go and live elsewhere and leave him in peace. All his emotional energy became concentrated on this one thought.

After several weeks of torment he began fantasising about how she'd take her own life, throw herself off the wharf and drown; even more bizarre, he would be the one to find her body. Fishing from that wharf as a boy while on holiday staying with his grandmother, he'd been fascinated by the way patches of sunlight sparkled on the water beneath his feet. It still surprised him how these areas were always brighter than he would have expected. And now he was convinced that one morning he'd discover her body floating there under the wharf.

The thought further increased his feelings of guilt. He even convinced himself that this desire for her death would somehow cause it to happen. Primitive thinking, clearly the omnipotent thoughts of someone much younger. He was losing his sanity, his mind constantly filled with thoughts of the Angry Woman – her death, his guilt. Edward desperately wanted to keep away from the wharf, but he was driven to it day after day by an irresistible urge to check for the body. Almost always she'd pass him long before he reached the wharf. Despite the knowledge that she was alive, he was compelled to proceed with his macabre inspection.

One day something occurred which made him feel physically ill. He came across the Angry Woman standing opposite the site where his grandmother's house had been. She was staring fixedly at the large house next door, now in a state of advanced disrepair. The thought flashed across his mind – could she have been *the child*? In the state he was in, Edward dared not comprehend the full meaning of what he was witnessing.

Sleep became impossible, he was losing weight, no longer having any interest in food. He knew he couldn't continue like this, but neither could he tell anyone. They might pronounce him mad, have him put away.

Then there was a respite, accompanied by a wonderful sense of relief! A day, two days, a week, three weeks, a full month, and finally *three months* passed without one sighting. She'd disappeared and he hadn't

176

found her body. Slowly Edward's confidence began to return. He gave up looking under the wharf, and his trip to the Himalayas once more became a possibility and began to occupy his thoughts. There were preparations to keep him busy, clothing to buy and background reading to do. He was delighted he could once more pick up a book and concentrate. He stepped up the length and pace of his walks looking for opportunities to do as much hill work as possible.

Returning from one of his longer walks, Edward once again found himself near the site of his grandmother's house. As he turned the corner beside the petrol station, there she was. A grotesque leer distorted her face, and she was coming straight for him not five paces distant!

She was two paces away, when her face suddenly changed. It became the face of an innocent child.

Sheer panic took hold.

In that instant Edward Kingsley, retired charted accountant, who had been cautious all his life, fled across the street and collided with a taxi.

Edward lay on his back staring at the cream-painted ceiling and green cotton curtaining surrounding the hospital bed, his entire world since the accident. Quadriplegia! If only his life had been snuffed out in that moment of horror.

When he was considered well enough Edward was visited by a young constable. The policeman reported that, other than the taxi driver, the only witness was a man who lived across the street. He'd been collecting mail at his front gate and was able to give a clear description of the whole incident. His statement said the elderly man had abruptly wheeled around and rushed in front of the oncoming vehicle. It appeared as if he had suddenly changed his mind. It had happened so quickly. There had definitely been no one else in sight.

The Samoan cab driver visited twice. He swore there wasn't a strange-looking woman on the pavement, no woman at all. The street had been deserted except for a man standing at his gate, and Edward.

# Sandshoes

If I died tomorrow there'd be nothing to remember me by. I'm what's called an ascetic – don't go in for owning lots of flash stuff. There's these sandshoes held together with pieces of string. I'm going to miss you, old friends. Mum made me buy a new pair. Nagged and nagged, threatening to buy me what she calls in her posh voice, 'A pair of proper shoes.'

Still, painting the new ones helped. I might just get attached to these little beauties. I'm sitting in the sun on the back doorstep, my favourite spot. With Mum and Dad away I've got the house to myself all weekend. Didn't get up till eleven. I've dined on my favourite breakfast – six Weet-Bix, cold milk and lots of sugar.

I painted them last night – that's the aesthetic side of me. I love the colours, the way they glisten in the sunshine when I hold them up and turn them around like this. Crimson, titanium white, ultramarine; red, white and blue. Yeah, I'm very sensitive to colour.

A tiny fleck of colour can trigger memories from way back. I saw a particular shade of green the other day and pictured myself in the new entrants' class cutting shapes out of shiny green flint-paper. And just yesterday I found a bird's egg on the front lawn, the exact colour of the bathroom tiles in the art-deco house we lived in years ago.

I pass the newly painted sandshoes under my nose and inhale. Smell, too, that's another thing I'm sensitive to. These acrylics have a sort of synthetic smell, not like watercolours or oils. I'm probably cut out to be an artist. I caress the shoes with the tips of my fingers, feeling the texture of new paint on canvas.

I bet Petra Davies would think these real sexy!

Yeah, an artist. Ascetic and aesthete, not a bad athlete either. Hah! Triple A rating me. Truth is, I'd do anything but this aimless grind at uni. Damn, that reminds me. The assignment. It's got to be in Monday before eleven, no extensions. 'Karl Marx as Sociologist' – and they reckon soc101 is a fluff subject. The thought ruins my day thinking about it. Bugger!

I'll toss it in. One day I'll just take off, go up north, get a job cutting scrub, earn a bit of dosh of my own. Won't have to feel beholden to the parents anymore. No deadlines, no responsibilities, give my brain a well-earned rest.

Then all unexpected, I'll turn up at a party bronzed and hardened. 'That's Rob Alexander isn't it? I'd like to feel those muscular arms around me, and look at those shoulders!' The best-looking girl in the room, Petra Davies, will sidle up to me. 'Where've you been all my life, stranger?' She's panting in my ear and I'm looking down at her perfect breasts beautifully displayed in a low-cut summer dress ...

Dad says I'm a dreamer, I'll show him. Someday I'll journey across a desert, just me against the forces of nature, barely enough food and water to keep me alive. From the Central Plateau across the Kaimanawas to Hawkes Bay, like that joker in the book we read in the seventh form. Shouldn't be too difficult. I was thinking of becoming a Trappist monk last year, but there'd be this little problem, what to do with my exceptionally strong sex drive? Most people wouldn't pick it just looking at me, how oversexed I am.

There's something about these shoes, though. What is it? I pick them up, turn them around a couple of times admiring the boldness of my artistry. Hold them up again so as they catch the sunlight. What? There's something not right, I can feel it in my gut. I measure the soles against each other.

'Fuck!' They're different! Different sizes! Bloody hell, the bastards have sold me a pair of shoes *and they're different sizes!* I stand up, about to fling the fuckers over the back fence, but restrain myself just in time.

Monday morning. I hobble into the shoe shop, my right foot squashed into a shoe that's too small. Just dropped off my assignment, made it with ten minutes to spare. I'm trying to get some attention now. That blond dusting the shelves looks bored out of her brain.

Quite a sultry look about her – not bad really.

'Excuse me, I bought these here on Friday, but after I got them home I found one's a size seven and the other's an eight.' I point to the shoes and begin taking them off. Whew! That's a relief.

'No, you can't have bought them here,' she puts her fluffy duster down and comes over for a closer look. 'We don't stock sandshoes with Union Jacks on them.'

'I know that, I painted them myself. Didn't notice the mistake till Saturday morning.'

'So. What d'you want us to do about it?'

'Well, I'd like another size eight which is my normal fitting. A size seven is far too small.' I'm feeling pain from a blister on top of my right big toe.

'I don't think we could do that, we have strict instructions never to break up pairs.' She's standing side on to me as she says it, accentuating her curves. No doubt about it – nice bum, great tits. Perhaps she fancies me, my animal magnetism.

'But if you went through your stock you might find the other odd pair – you know, a seven and an eight.'

'No, that couldn't happen, we always sell pairs that are the same size.' She's saying this with a wide-eyed, unblinking, dumb look on her face.

'You sold *me* an odd pair!' I'm getting nowhere. Better keep my cool. 'Could I speak to the manager about this?'

'Just a moment. I'll go see if he's available.' She wiggles her bottom at me as she heads out the back.

She's back. She's climbing a small set of steps. There's

no doubt about it that miniskirt shows off her lovely little bum, and a great pair of legs. Almost as good as Petra Davies. Pity she's such a dummy otherwise I'd ask her out. Where's that manager? Meantime, I might just sidle over to the rack by the entrance where they've got the sandshoes.

They all look like pairs. I've recently developed super-sensitive eyesight and judgement when it comes to spotting differences in sandshoes. Shortly I'll be getting my hands on one of those size eights. Planning ahead now, the mark of a master crook. With my back to the blond, I carefully untie the laces holding one of the pairs together.

God, but I hate shopping, so depressing, usually try to avoid it like the plague. I know exactly where that's coming from, being dragged all over town by Mum when I was a kid. She's a shopping freak, always poking about, picking up this, picking up that, trying stuff on. You can bet on it, that manager's waiting out the back trying to unnerve me. And, he's succeeded.

Here he comes now, small and dark with a thin pointy face, and nattily dressed. And he's wearing very shiny shoes. Oh God, I groan inwardly. I amble back to the counter.

'How can we help you, *sir?*'

'I bought these here on Friday and when I got home I noticed one's size seven and the other's an eight.'

The manager lowers his horn-rimmed glasses which have been parked on his coiffured head. He peers at the sandshoes sitting on the counter, clears his throat and intones. 'These shoes have been painted with what appear to be Union Jacks.'

'Yes, well, I painted them before I noticed they're different sizes. Don't you normally sell pairs of shoes in the same size?'

'I'm afraid there's nothing we can do about this, *sir!* Company policy is crystal clear on the subject. Stock that has been worn, interfered with, altered or embellished in any way cannot be replaced.' He's droning on through his nose.

'But you people made the mistake selling me an odd pair. I'm sure there must be a law against that.'

'I've stated our company's policy, which I assure you complies with the letter of the law in every respect. Look.' He's reaching under the desk. 'Here's the comp-any's manual – I'll show you the relevant clause.'

'Don't bother.' I'm getting nowhere. 'If that's your last word on the subject you can expect to hear from my solicitor.'

That sounded pretty impressive. I pick up the shoes and move toward the door. The blond bit is still up the ladder stifling a giggle. I'm alongside the rack of sandshoes, I pause momentarily, lean ever so slightly extending my left arm. My hand closes around the size eight I'd previously selected. I stuff it down my shirt, and at the same time with my right hand I'm hurling the Union Jack size seven over my shoulder as hard as I can, hoping it'll hit the prick with the shiny shoes fair smack in his prissy little gob!

And I'm out that door clutching my Union Jack size

eight, going at top. Shite! Why did I do that? I can feel the new size eight bouncing around inside my shirt. A second's hesitation is followed by a terrific feeling of power. First time in my life I've stolen anything, but this is Robin Hood stuff, completely justified whichever way you look at it.

*You're a hard-case surprise, Rob Alexander. You'd have been a highwayman in the olden days, all the women falling for you* ... Petra Davies. She's not only a terrific looker, she's intelligent as well.

There's no way I can keep this up – running in bare feet. Home's easily three kilometres from here. If I take some back streets I can slow down. You never know, he might be following in a car, or perhaps he's phoned the cops. Bit of a worry that. I can hear a car coming now, it's getting closer – slowing down – not a good sign. I'd better not look back, the action of a guilty party.

Alongside! Oh God, it's slowed right down to a crawl.

'Say, fellah, d'yah know where Adam Terrace is?'

Just another taxi.

'Sorry, mate, I don't live round here.'

The working classes overthrowing the yoke of capitalism. I think I might ditch the idea of doing religious studies next year. Political science, that's got to be it. This sort of exploitation of the poor by the rich is completely immoral. What about the law? Nah, law favours the establishment. The whole system needs overhauling and I'm going to be part of that revolution. Ouch! My feet are hurting like crazy. It's probably safe to walk for a bit.

I'm out of the danger zone, back in the posh area where my parents live. Time I moved out. I'll get a room in some rundown part of town. I've been feeling uncomfortable for a long time, living with all that affluence.

I reach home and go straight to my room. Haul the stolen shoe from inside my shirt. A blank canvas, can't wait to get my paints onto it. First, though, I'll try it on … this new little beauty …

What!! Flaming Hell! They're both left feet!

After all that, I've pinched myelf another left shoe. I want to cry. I cry. But not for long. I giggle. I'm pissing myself. I slide off the bed onto the floor tears streaming down my face. I'm clutching the shoes to my chest, both of them bloody left feet. I'm rolling around like an idiot. Fuck, what a dag!

*You're a character, Rob, got a wonderful sense of humour*. Petra Davies strokes my biceps. I can see her nipples through that low-cut dress, and whaddya know, she's not wearing a bra!

But let's face it, Petra Davies is never going to look at me. And as for leaving home – what, with no money? Going off up north, yeah, get off a bus in the middle of nowhere, tramp around asking farmers for work. Can't see myself doing that. Dad could be right about me being a dreamer.

What am I going to do for shoes now? Fuck! I'll have to ask Mum for money to buy another pair. You won't catch me going back to that shop with the little fart of a manager. I'd quite like to see Blondie again though. I might just hang around across the road some time, around 5.30, that's probably when she knocks off, I reckon. See if the old animal magnetism's still working.

# Fantail

Friday, 5pm. We're on our way.

'So you drongos think you're going to shoot some deers.' Jacko's in the back seat of the Roast. 'I bet none of youse been hunting before.'

'No bastard said I had,' replies Stevie, gripping the wheel on a slight bend. 'The bloody steering's a bit sloppy on this old jalopy – heh, heh!'

Mel owns the car but Stevie's having a turn driving.

'What about you, Melopuff? You're keepin' very quiet about your effing hunting prowess,' says Jacko.

'Ah, shut it, yah bloody cretin.' Mel's beside Stevie on the bench seat of the green 1948 Ford Prefect. You may remember that basic straight-up-and-down job. Looks as if they'd tip over if you cornered too fast. He's occupied opening another bottle of Red Band.

'Yeah, Jacko,' said Mel, 'I bet you've never done any hunting either.'

'Listen, I've shot more deers than you bastards have … aw, go to hell! Well, maybe not deer, pigs anyway.'

'Oh, yeah, about as believable as all those sheilas yer reckon yer've shagged.'

'Have so bloody, too.' Jacko's getting talkative. 'When I was a kid I used to go pig hunting on me uncle's farm up the King Country. Often went after pig, used to stick the little buggers. Got charged once by this friggin' great boar. The dogs had the bastard bailed up against a tree when it breaks loose and makes a run for it, coming straight at me.'

'So let's hear it, what did Hiawatha do next?' Stevie's grabbing the bottle of beer off Mel and taking a long swig. With his head tilted right back it's impossible for him to see the road. Mel tenses, looks straight ahead as his right hand reaches toward the wheel.

Jacko's continuing, oblivious to the danger. 'Well the fucker's coming straight for me, so I whips out me trusty pocket knife, do this dodgy little sidestep just like Freddie Allen. Then, as this fucking great boar rushes past, I lean down and slit the bastard's throat – blood and guts everywhere.'

'Not very original I'm afraid, Jacko,' says Mel.

'What a load of bullshit! Here, give the man a drink,' Stevie's passing the bottle over his shoulder. 'I reckon that bit of Hollywood's worth a glug or two.'

'Hey! Watch it!' says Jacko. 'You turn up here. Now head straight for the hills, matey. I bet those deers would be shitting themselves if they knew what's in bloody store for them. Fuckin' deer slayers, one for all and all for one! Shit, I think I might have had a few too many.'

Jacko's leaning over from the back seat, his permanently red, peeling nose is glowing like a beacon between the other two up front.

'You're not going to chunder, not in my car,' says Mel. 'Hey Stefano, stop the Sunday Roast, the cheapo drunk in the back's about to chunder down your neck.'

'Not bloody likely. I'll be is right is rain, soon as I get into the bush on the tail of those liddle bambis,' slurs Jacko.

Another few miles and the gravel turns into clay wheel tracks. Mānuka, blackberry and broom brush the sides of the car. They arrive at the riverbed. The river is amber in colour, quite shallow, and flows gently down the middle of a broad stretch of boulders and gravel, dotted here and there with patches of sand.

'Trev said we park here and hoof it upstream to the whare,' says Mel.

'That'll be the day. You won't catch me luggin' all this gear. And what about the beer, and the grub? Listen, Mel, the old Roast can handle that stuff no sweat.' Steve indicates the rock and shingle in the riverbed. 'This little fucker'd go anywhere – betcha! What do you say, Jacko?'

'Right on, sport. Give her the herbs, Stefano me ol' mate.'

'Hold it! If anyone's going to drive it'll be me. All very well for you bastards, but it's not your car.'

Mel's shoving her into first and heading upstream. It's a bumpy ride for several hundred metres, the car bucking around, slewing sideways as it slips off the river boulders. Twice they get stuck in sandy patches requiring Jacko and Steve to jump out and push; and a few times Mel has to back up and have another go when the front wheels get jammed against large rocks.

'That'll be the whare over there.'

They focus on the little hut sitting in a small clearing. It's surrounded by dense bush with a few large beech trees here and there.

'Nice one, Melo. The trusty Roast, knew she could do it.'

'And what if it rains tonight and the river rises – what then? Why do I ever listen to you bastards?' Mel gets out and surveys the area, looking for some higher ground. He decides where the car is now is as good as anywhere, and, it's pretty close to the whare. 'Are we going to get this beast unloaded, or aren't we?' They make a couple of trips with the gear, borrowed rifles, food and two crates of beer.

'For Christ's sake, Stephen, did you buy this grub?' Mel's looking inside the food carton. 'We're in for some variety, aren't we? All I can see here are cans of spaghetti and three loaves of bread, not even any butter! Are you off your head? If you want to put me in a bad mood you're sure going the right way about it.

'Well you buy the fucking food next time. At least I brought a fucking can opener.'

'I don't think there's going to be a next time, if you

wankers can't do any better than this.'

All three are examining the whare. Even the roof is ponga, a good half of it has fallen in at the fireplace end which is hopelessly wet and clogged with rubbish. The pongas glisten with moisture inside as well as out, and permanent droplets of dew cling to dozens of little spider webs. On one side, there's a heap of debris which had once been a couple of cots constructed of sacking and mānuka stakes. In the driest corner someone has piled ponga fronds, now turned brown and brittle. Driving up the riverbed there'd been talk of a cosy little hut with bunks and a blazing fire.

'Jesus,' says Stevie. 'Not exactly home away from home, is it?'

Mel suggests they get a fire going to heat up some spag' before it gets dark. Sticks of green whitey wood hiss and smoke, but no amount of blowing raises more than a temporary flicker, and soon the whare is filled with the acrid vegetable smell of māhoe smoke. They eat the cold spaghetti with sliced bread and down a bottle of beer each.

'I think I'll join the army,' says Jacko. 'The food's got to be better than this shit.'

'And I think I might join you,' says Mel.

As darkness arrives and the chilly night air seeps in, no amount of moaning and blaming can keep the noises and shadows of the forest at bay.

'Whose fucking idea was this trip anyway,' says Mel. This is the last hunting trip I'm going on with you no-hopers!'

'Yeah, I seem to remember it was your fucking brother, Trev, who told us about *the neat little whare*,' says Steve.

'So. It's more than a couple of years since he's been in here. You can hardly blame Trev.'

'Let's play spin the bottle,' suggests Jacko.

'Nah, Russian roulette. Though with my rotten luck, I'd sure as hell end up not blowing my bloody brains out,' says Mel.

They play spin the bottle by candlelight, and their senses become progressively dulled by the quantity of beer consumed.

'I'm gunna shoot the candle out,' says Jacko. He's on his feet with the rifle up to his shoulder. He discharges two rounds, missing the candle every time, before the other two can restrain him.

'For Christ's sake,' says Mel. 'Put that bloody thing away before you kill someone.'

They attempt to settle for the night, but discover there's insufficient room for all three at the drier end of the whare.

'I'm going to sleep in the Roast,' says Mel.

'I bags the back seat,' says Steve.

'And you can get stuffed,' says Mel. 'It's my car, have the front seat or nothing.'

Stevie spends the night doubled up, with shoulders jammed against the steering wheel and legs hanging sideways off the passenger seat. Mel has the best of it in the back and manages a few hours broken sleep. Jacko feels justified in downing another bottle of Red Band as he contemplates the others luxuriating in the car.

Dawn comes eventually: still, cold, with mist right down in the valley. Stevie's up first. He fires a shot over the whare, and another over the car. Their eyes are red-rimmed and swollen. No one bothers trying to light a fire. Another tin of spag' each and three slices of bread. Stevie moans about the chilly beer.

The territory's divided up. Steve gets the right side of the valley heading upstream, Mel the left-hand side, and Jacko's awarded the entire area below the whare where the terrain is relatively flat. Mel and Steve suspect Jacko's block holds less promise than the slopes further up. Mel instructs the other two on positively identifying any target before firing. He's remembered that much from Trev's little pep talk.

Despite the cold, Mel's relieved to get into the bush and away from the other two plonkers.

By mid-morning the sun's starting to show through the cloud, and here and there it filters into the bush, lifting Mel's spirits. He's been treading carefully and quietly through the bush, keeping alert for any signs or sounds. It's quite tiring he finds, doing a circuit which takes him up to a ridge where the beech trees open out. It's a good place to have a rest with his back against a tree. Mel digs into a pocket of Trev's Swanndri jacket, which he's borrowed, and finds some tobacco, matches and cigarette papers. As he rolls a smoke, he realises he's covered this area about three times already, and he hasn't come across anything to have a shot at. Perhaps he'll have a little target practice.

There's a fantail, which has been flitting around catching insects. It is perched on a twig halfway up a tree – about twenty paces away. No, it's flying around again. Without giving it a moment's thought Mel stands, raises the rifle to his shoulder, aims, and fires. He hasn't got a show in hell from a standing position at that distance. But it's a complete fluke shot, collecting the little bird and smashing it to pieces. Feathers and bits of body everywhere.

'Mel, what have you done, you bloody sicko?' He's spoken out loud. He's killed a poor defenceless bird. 'You're a sicko, Mel, a bloody sicko.'

Mel puts down the firearm and crawls around collecting up fragments of body and feathers, which are scattered over a couple of square metres. He scrapes out a shallow grave beneath the tree the bird was flying around only a couple of minutes earlier. Placing the remains in the little grave, he covers it over with a pile of leaves.

'Please forgive me, little bird,' he prays.

Mel recalls the old Māori woman who lived next door when he was a small kid. Mrs Tangiora had told him that fantails, or pīwakawaka as she called them, always herald the presence of death. Mel had been on the verge of tears when he buried the bird, and now he is overcome with feelings of guilt and fear. He begins to recite a string of Hail Marys as he picks up the rifle and leaves the scene of his crime.

Twenty minutes later, wandering along still feeling rotten and still breaking into a few Hail Marys, he comes across a deer in a small clearing, no more than eight metres away. Mel has never seen a deer before, when suddenly here is this majestic animal standing real close, looking straight at him. He knows it must be a doe, he remembers that word, because of the size of her belly. She is in fawn. Mel notices her colour, browny-grey, and the wet nose and bulging eyes. A tiny plume of steam rises off her nose as her jaw moves sideways. She is swallowing what would be her last mouthful of sapling. Mel slowly raises his rifle, watching through the sights. He pulls the trigger when the barrel is pointed three feet above the doe's head. CRACK!

'Now, bugger off!'

The doe swivels around with head down, crashes through the undergrowth, down a bank, and heads up the valley. Mel hopes she'll continue in that direction, as far away from his mates as possible.

There is absolutely no way he is going to tell Steve and Jacko, or anyone else, why he fired the first shot, and the second as well. Why he baulked at killing the deer.

Arriving back he's confronted by Jacko and Stevie fast asleep in a patch of sun beside the whare. 'Heh! Wake up you lazy bastards, been asleep for hours I suppose.'

Jacko comes to. 'Gidday, chief, that must have been you banging away up there. Two shots, two deers, straight through the eyeball. Yeah, just like that.'

Stevie, who had almost no sleep in the front seat

of the car, gradually comes round. 'Where's all the venison, Mel? I've been dreaming of a big roast of venison, baked spuds, kūmara, peas and beans – the lot.'

'Sorry fellahs, there ain't any. Not quite, anyway, had a crack at a big stag – would've been a fourteen pointer at least – way over on a ridge above the next valley. It was a hell of a long shot.'

'Yeah, right,' the other two say in unison.

The lads had enough of hunting, and the thought of another night in the bush holds no appeal. They load the Roast, head back along the riverbed, and up to the sealed road.

'Hey you drongos, how about we play spider?' It's Stevie's suggestion.

'Nah, stupid idea,' says Mel.

'Are yah chicken then?' says Jacko.

Mel finally relents under pressure. 'Only on the flat, though, not over the hill. Now I mean that.'

'You grab the steering, Jacko, seeing you can't reach the pedals from over there,' says Steve.

'I dunno,' says Jacko. 'I could poke the pedals with me rifle.'

'Or your stupid nose,' says Stevie. 'Don't be ridiculous – you're steering.'

'I'll have the accelerator and the clutch,' says Mel. 'Stevie, you take the stick. You'll have to tell me when to push the clutch pedal.'

Mel's checking everything off in his head. Steering, accelerator, clutch, stick. That ought to cover it …

'Right you fellahs, we're off!' says Steve.

'The deer slayers return!' shouts Jacko. 'And don't forget to stop at the Featherston fucking pub!'

Mel pushes the acelerator pedal, and the clutch when Stevie gives him the word. But he's not really into the sport, his mind is elsewhere still feeling bad about the little fantail, and remembering what old Mrs Tangiora said. He's desperately trying to hold a picture in his head of the beautiful deer. Sparing the deer's life must count for something.

'And watch the steering on this corner, Jacko! Remember it's a bit shagged. *Jacko!*'

The truck driver at the inquest said he saw the little green car coming toward him, veering across the centre line. There were legs and heads everywhere. It was impossible to tell, in the split-second before the crash, who was driving.

# Digger

Shivers, the curtain's moving! Could be a burglar trying to get in through the top window. Mum wouldn't make me keep it open if only she knew how much it gives me the creeps. She's always going on about how it's unhealthy not to have fresh air coming in. Mustn't move – hold my breath! – this is real scary. It's always scarier after she's asleep. I used to get to sleep before Mum went to bed, not lately though.

The curtain's stopped. Phew. He must have taken off. Everything's gone wrong lately. If only she'd let me get all my hair cut off, maybe Bruce would still be alive. Poppa told me about these kids who got all their hair shaved off, so they'd look like their friend who had the horrible blood disease, like Bruce. Mum said she wanted to think about that, but Bruce went back into hospital three weeks ago, and then he died almost straight away.

The curtain's moving again. That burglar's back. I suppose it could just be the wind blowing it out like that. They said he died in his sleep, said it was a lovely way for him to go. *Died in his sleep.* How do I know I won't die in my sleep? How do I know I haven't got some horrible disease that nobody knows about, and it's slowly killing me? And one night, maybe tonight, I'll die in my sleep too – just won't wake up in the morning.

I'd better try to think of something else.

Dad used to pick me up every Saturday, but I haven't seen him for weeks. He'd know how to deal with a burglar. I bet Poppa would too. Poppa's neat, he calls me Digger, or sometimes just Dig. 'Gidday, Dig,' he says. He reckons I'm amazing the way I dig these great big holes in our back garden. Poppa says it's got to be in my blood. He was telling me how he used to be a coal miner and a rock tunneller. He said I could be a coal miner or a rock tunneller when I grow up, but then he said there wasn't much scope these days. I wonder what he meant by that. Uncle Matt showed me his new hunting rifle the other day, and that's got a scope.

Poppa said how he was an explosives' expert, which meant he used to blow up enormous chunks of coal or rock so other men could load it onto the wagons. That would be great, blowing things up. Sometimes I'd like to blow up the whole world; well, perhaps not everyone, just the people I hate. Perhaps an explosives expert has a scope like on Uncle Matt's rifle, so he can watch the blast from a long way off, out of danger. That'll be it. Maybe there's not enough scopes to go round. Everything's hard to get these days.

Geez! What if I drop off to sleep and then don't wake up like Bruce. They'll all be real sad – especially Dad, cause he hasn't taken me out lately. He'll be at the side of the grave as they lower my coffin into the big hole, like they did with Bruce. Mum and Dad will be standing there together holding hands, just like Bruce's mum and dad. Dad'll cry and say he's sorry for all those times he's promised to come round and hasn't. And Mum'll blub and say that if Dad hadn't gone to live with that Sharon, I'd still be alive, cause Dad would have been here to fight off the burglar that murdered me. Or, I might have died of the blood disease. They'd be feeling really, really, really sorry.

You couldn't tell Bruce had the blood disease except for going bald and being a bit on the small side for his age. Some people call me a shrimp, could that mean …?

Tomorrow's Saturday, at least I won't have to get up so early. The teacher told Mum I was looking tired lately. And that's another thing, Bruce was always tired in the weeks before he died. I'll have to think of something else, otherwise I'll never get to sleep.

Tomorrow I'll finish off the latest hole I'm digging. I might get some boards and make a roof and put some boxes in it for furniture. Maybe some of the other kids might come round and help me finish it off. Probably not, though, they'll be playing on their mountain bikes, or with Shane's laptop like they always do. I asked Mum for a bike for Christmas, but she said she couldn't afford it now she's on the benefit. She's always using that as an excuse for not getting me stuff like the other kids have. Dad used to get me things sometimes, but not lately, not since he went to live with Sharon and those kids of hers.

I'd better try to get to sleep. What can I think about? I know – Dad turns up tomorrow morning and says, 'Let's go, Jamie, we'll go to McDonalds for lunch, and then we'll go see *The Lion King*. How'd you like that? By the way I've left Sharon and those brats and I'm coming back to live with you and Mum, and this Christmas we'll go on a proper holiday – camping, put up the tent beside a river with a beaut swimming hole, like the one in Nelson Graham told you about! That'd be great, wouldn't it?'

I'm sitting up my tree. Everyone calls it Jamie's tree. It's a big, ugly old pine in the back corner, right on the boundary of our section. It's tall and bushy, untidy looking, not like the ones that grow straight up. It's been my tree ever since I was quite small, ever since I learned to climb. That was a long time ago. Dad used to have to lift me up to the first branch. My dad isn't as big and strong now as he was back then. I love my tree. The thing I like best is the way it helps me when I'm sad or angry.

I made this platform by nailing some boards between two of the branches, and when I sit up here with my back to the trunk and it's swaying in the wind, it soothes me, sort of smoothes my mind. I like the smell of the pine needles too, but I don't like the sticky stuff that gets on my hands. Mum goes mad if I get it on my clothes.

I've got a secret saying for my tree which I sometimes say out loud when no one's around to hear. It's something like the psalm I learned when I used to go to Sunday School: 'I will lift up my eyes to the tree from where comes my strength.' I've been saying it over and over and over, but it's not working today. It's not helping my angry feelings one little bit. I've been thinking about my dad. I love my dad but he still hasn't taken me out, and it's been weeks and weeks now.

'Bloody, bloody, bloody, buggers, bugger, bugger, buggers!' I'm shouting from the very top of my tree. And I don't care who hears. Mum will be out soon saying, 'Jamie, you stop that swearing! Whatever will the neighbours think?'

What made me really mad was when Sharon's kids came up to me at school yesterday. Those cheeky brats told me about the neat time they'd had with my dad. *My* dad! 'Bloody, bloody, bloody, buggers, buggers, buggers!'

Saying that made me feel a bit better. Sometimes I've thought about jumping off the top of my tree when Mum's watching. That'd give them a fright. It's not that I'd hurt myself, well, not badly anyway, the branches would hold me as I fall, sort of bump me down to the ground. I can trust this old tree.

Anyway, I haven't been worried about dying, not

since I worked out my plan. It's a secret plan so I can't tell anyone, especially not the adults, they might laugh and say it wouldn't work. I have to believe in my plan so I won't die.

Mum asked me why I was digging all these holes that look like graves. She said it made her feel sick when she looked out the kitchen window. I couldn't tell her the truth, could I? She'd only get in a tizzy again. It was when things were really bad, and I was hardly getting any sleep at all. I was sitting up here in my tree thinking about all these problems and worries, and that's when I got the great idea, my secret plan. It goes like this ...

When people die, they need someone to dig the graves. Right? I, Jamie, will become a champion at digging graves, but I'll need to practice real hard. I'll become a professional gravedigger, which means I'll get paid for it too. And I'll become so good, people just won't be able to do without me.

And the most important part of my plan – I won't be able to die myself, so I can go on digging graves for everybody else. The famous gravedigger will have to be kept alive to dig other people's graves.

Yes, it's working, my worries have jolly nearly disappeared. I'm looking down and admiring 'my handiwork', as Poppa would say. From up here my graves look pretty nearly perfect – a whole row of them stretching right across the back of our section. With all this practice I'm getting to be really good at digging. Poppa says I've got digging in my genes. I think he means that I've inherited it from him, from when he was a coal miner and a rock tunneller.

I think I'm going to sing you a little song I've made up. I've been singing it a lot lately, especially when I'm sitting up my tree. It goes a bit like 'Farmer in the Dell'.

'I'm the World's Greatest Gravedigger,
the World's Greatest Gravedigger,
the Greatest Gravedigger the World has ever seen!'

# Acknowledgements

Norman Bilbrough for his Saturday morning creative writing course, which I attended many moons ago. My wife, Judith, for her ideas, support and inspiration. Mary McCallum of Mākaro Press, for her astute insights, meticulous attention to detail, positive attitude, and belief in me.